HOT NANNY NEXT DOOR

CATHRYN FOX

ISBN Ebook: 978-1-989374-45-0

ISBN Print: 978-1-989374-44-3

ANNA

My phone pings in my purse but I work to ignore it as I hurry through the busy grocery store. I try to keep my focus, try desperately to keep my eyes on the list crushed in my palm, but I can't stop glancing over my shoulder. Any second now I expect my father's big, burly hand to clamp down on my shoulder—not to hurt me, but to drag me home.

Running away might not have been my smartest move, but being sheltered for eighteen long years, my every movement scrutinized, meant I had no other options available. I needed to act fast if I wanted to stop my family from marrying me off to some guy I've never met and know nothing about, other than his last name is Ivanov. I refuse to be a pawn in their game, a means to bring two powerful mafia families together. That was the line in the sand for me, and what drove me to run away from home, and disappear under the cover of darkness.

It's surprising I wasn't caught. But it's a miracle I'm not going to question. Honestly, how can both my mother and father think feeding me to the wolves is a good idea? Sure, they had an arranged marriage, and they are both heavily involved in the underworld, but it's not for me. I've told them that numerous times. They simply won't listen.

I smooth out the long list in my shaky hand—the items I need scribbled on the finest of stationery—and rush through the produce section. I need half a dozen apples. Green ones, to be precise. I haven't been working for the Castello family long enough to know what kind of wrath they'd bring down upon me if I brought home the wrong color apple for their daughter Sophie, the sweet little girl I've been taking care of for the last week.

I maneuver my big cart through the crowd, find the display of green apples and reach for one. The second I do, my hand connects with warm fingers. Warm fingers that lead to a big hand and thick arm. My gaze slides up from the fingers, noticing the impressive arm attached to a very broad shoulder. My gaze lifts higher, to discover all those body parts belong to a very handsome man who looks like he could command a room without even trying. A man like the men who work for my father. I gasp and jerk my arm back.

His dark eyes narrow in on me, and I try not to shift under his scrutiny. Sweat breaks out on my forehead, despite the air conditioning in the grocery store, and my heart crashes a little harder against my ribs as I give him another once over. Tall. Foreboding. Powerful. He represents everything I've been running from.

Is this one of my father's men? Have they found me already? I'd been so careful, so secretive the last few weeks. Using burner phones each time I called the Practically Perfect Nannies in search of a job. Thanks to my mixed heritage—I can speak English and Italian fluently—I was promptly placed with a Sicilian family who wanted me to teach their daughter English and still be able to communicate with them all in Italian. While Chicago's Gold Coast is gorgeous, I would have preferred a place a little further from my home, but I was desperate, so I jumped on it, being careful to keep a low profile until I can save up enough to get out of Chicago altogether.

Then I can go to college like I want, instead of marrying at eighteen. I have my whole life ahead of me. I want to experience things, to travel, and hopefully someday own my own restaurant. I could have asked my father for college money, but he'd want me married first. Once married, he'd tell me I didn't need an education. In the world I was born into, it's still an old fashioned one, where the men rule the roost. I'm a modern woman and want a life in the modern world.

"Are you okay?" the man asks as he smooths a big hand down his tie. I follow the movement. I take a breath, and then another, working to pull myself together long enough to find my voice.

"Yes, sorry." I point to the apples as I work to figure out if this man is going to drag me from the store by my hair. From the way people are giving him a wide berth, I don't even think they'd try to stop him. "You go ahead."

I size him up again. I've gotten good at reading others over the years. Who is friend and who is foe? Everything about him, from his expensive suit and shoes to his perfectly shaven face and combed hair—that wouldn't dare to tumble out of place—screams wealth and power. He's everything I despise. Guys like him rule the world, telling girls like me what to do and how to do it. I am so over that, and truth be told, I'm a little surprised he's getting his own groceries. You'd think a man in a suit that costs thousands of dollars would have servants, and many of them. Unless, of course, he's one of my father's henchmen, buying groceries under pretense, when he's actually here for me.

"No, you go ahead." He checks his watch. "You seem to be in a rush. I have a few minutes to spare."

I hesitate for a second and narrow my eyes. Is he waiting for backup? As I study his handsome chiseled face, recognition niggles in the back of my brain. Do I know him? Have I met him before? If he's not one of my father's men, he could be from a rival family, keeping his eye on me. Arianna Milano. Though I've changed it to Miller to keep my identity hidden. The prized little virgin who can bring the Sicilian and Russian mafia together.

My virginity is not for sale, thank you very much.

As I look at this man, take in his gorgeous face and hard body made for sin, a devious thought hits like a lightning bolt. If I gave my virginity away to a stranger, maybe I wouldn't be so valuable to my family, or so coveted by their rivals.

"Are you okay?" he asks again as I stand there and size up his body and hands, imagining what they'd feel like on my naked body.

Move, Anna. Get what you need and get out.

I snatch up six apples and he stands there, towering over me as I juggle the apples, struggling to open the stupid plastic bag. I am not about to lick my fingers. God knows what kind of germs linger in grocery stores.

"Here let me help you." His big hand once again brushes mine as he takes the bag away from me, and rage wells up inside me. I am not a stupid little girl who can't do things for herself. I was just never allowed the freedom to try anything.

"I've got it," I snap and snatch it back. He frowns at me, and my chest tightens. Why am I getting mad at him? He was only trying to help and if he's not here to collect me and I'm just being paranoid, there is no reason for him to be the brunt of the anger that's been building inside me for years. "I'm sorry. I shouldn't be taking my bad mood out on you."

"You don't have to be sorry. If you want to open your own bag, you should open your own bag." He steps back and waves his hand.

I smile at him as I turn toward the display. "Thanks."

"Grab it by the handles." He leans into me, his breath warm on my neck. "It's easier to open from there."

I do as he suggests and peel the plastic open. "Thanks for the tip." I fill the bag, and once again, I look over my shoulder. Not for my father, but something about this guy draws me in. He's everything I hate in a man, yet I can't seem to stop staring at him. He checks something on his phone as I tie my bag and set it in my cart. He reaches for his own plastic bag, but I get to it first. I rub the plastic together, and open it for him.

He chuckles. "Thanks."

"Can I...uh...ask for another tip?"

He goes quiet, like he's contemplating my request as he picks up a big green apple, sizes it up, and drops it into his bag. "Sure."

"Do you have any tips for buying watermelon? I saw a guy knocking on one for a good solid minute." I laugh. "I was about to tell him I didn't think anyone was home."

He stares at me like I might have two heads, then he bursts out laughing. His deep voice garners the attention of others, but they all avert their gazes when I glance at them. What the hell is that all about? They're acting like they're afraid of me.

His laughter dies down, and he says, "Have you never been to a grocery store before?"

I'm also a little embarrassed to admit it, but this is my first time. We always had servants do the shopping, cleaning, and anything else considered menial labor. Now I'm doing all those things for the Castello family.

"Do you always shop in an expensive suit?" I shoot back, not wanting to answer.

He angles his head, eyes me with a curious grin on his face. "I just flew in. I was away on business. Green apples are my son's favorite. I wanted to bring him home something special."

Oh, so he's married. Not like it matters, and who knew all kids liked green apples so much.

"No chocolate, no junk food?"

He frowns at me, and I lean in conspiratorially, although I have no idea why I'm acting all friendly like this. I don't know who this man is, and he could be the enemy. "When you were a five-year-old boy, what did you like?"

"Five-year-old girls," he says, and I can't help but laugh. He smiles with me.

"Seriously. Did your mother give you apples when you wanted a treat?"

"Okay, fine. What would you suggest?"

I glance around and consider it. "Popsicles."

He nods, like he can get behind that. "Okay. But he really does love green apples. As for popsicles, I used to like those rocket ones. There was this ice cream truck that used to drive down the street in our neighborhood." He grins like he has such fond memories, and to be honest, I'm a bit jealous. "They had three colors. What were they, red, white and green?"

"Not green, blue."

"I'm pretty sure it was green."

"Maybe you're color blind."

"I am not..." He shakes his head and laughs. "Okay, maybe I am a bit." This time he leans into me conspiratorially. "Are you going to tell me?"

My body stiffens. "Tell you what?" I ask, once again aware that I shouldn't be talking to strange men who could be under my father's control.

"Have you never been to a grocery store before?"

"Ah, no. I mean yes," I say quickly. "I...just, never bought watermelon before."

There's a spark of amusement in his dark eyes as the fib spills from my lips. He doesn't believe me.

You are lying, Anna.

Instead of calling me on it, he says, "It's to check the water content. Come here I'll show you how to do it, uh..." He moves toward the bin overflowing with huge watermelon, and lets his words fall off and I get it, he's waiting for my name.

"Anna." He arches a brow, waiting for me to continue, and I say. "It's just Anna."

"Okay, Anna." He picks up a watermelon and puts it in my hand. "Knock on it. If it makes a hollow sound, it's ripe and ready." As soon as the words leave his mouth, his gaze drops, takes in the V in my t-shirt, and a wave of warmth races through me. Is he wondering if I'm ripe and ready? God, men are so disgusting.

I tap on the watermelon, but I can't tell if it's making a hollow sound. He fishes around the bin, tapping on melons, and comes out with one. "Listen to the difference." He taps, and I tap. We repeat this a couple times, and he says, "Now all we need is a guitarist."

I laugh at his joke and set the watermelon into my basket. "I think this is a good one. Thanks for your help."

"Anytime, Anna."

My name rumbles from the depths of his throat, and I'm not sure what it is, but I really like the way it rolls off his tongue, like he's tasting it, testing the sound in his ears. He turns from me, and the next thing I know, he's gone from the produce section. I didn't get his name, but it doesn't matter. I'll likely never set eyes on him again. Strange. He's big and commanding, everything I hate in a guy, yet I have an odd sense of disappointment in my gut that our conversation has ended.

The last thing you need is that type of man in your life, Anna.

I shake my head to clear it, rush around the store to finish my shopping and head to the front to pay. Once done, I make my way outside, the mid-August sun shining down on me. I wheel the cart to my car, load it, and just as I'm about to put it back, the hairs on the back of my neck tingle.

I do a slow sweep of the parking lot. An SUV drives past, the driver a middle-aged woman, singing along to some song on the radio completely ignoring me. As she passes, my gaze lands on a very expensive sports car. I recognize the Maserati because my father owns one. It speeds off before I can see who the driver is, but my gut tells me it was Mr. Hot Produce Guy himself.

Worry once again invades my brain, and I jump into the driver's seat. Mrs. Castello lent me her vehicle. It's not a Maserati, but it's still a very nice sporty BMW.

I hurry back to the house and quickly unload the groceries. The family is out this afternoon, but will expect dinner when they get home. I glance at the clock. If I hurry, I can get a swim in before I have to start cooking.

I dart to my room and grab my bathing suit. I've lost weight I couldn't spare over the last couple of weeks. That's what stress will do to the body. I guess no one is around to see me in my loose bikini anyway. I make my way outside, stand at the end of the pool, and dive in. Coolness washes over me, but once again, I get the strange feeling that I'm being watched. I surface at the far end of the pool, and that's when I notice movement in the window next door. I stand quickly, peering into the neighbor's upstairs window, my heart beating a little faster.

Was that...the guy from the grocery store.

As I puzzle that out, I realize that might not be the worst of my problems. No, the fact that my bikini top shifted, and I might have just flashed Mr. Hot Produce Guy—the Castellos' neighbor—could end up with me getting fired.

FML.

2

ALEK

Sweet Jesus.

I try to tear my gaze away, really, I do. But the lush sight before me is so goddamn mouthwatering it makes it hard to remember I'm a gentleman. Which I am. Most times, anyway. Or never.

What the hell is Anna doing in my neighbor's pool? Talk about a coincidence, which I don't believe in. Everything happens for a reason, yet I don't understand the reason behind us bumping into each other at the grocery store, or why she's flashing me from the neighbor's pool. Did they hire help when I was in Atlanta consulting with a client? They talked about it before, but were always too afraid to leave Sophie with anyone, considering she has special needs, and Anna, well she doesn't even look like she's out of high school yet. All the more reason for me to back the fuck away from my window, and the illict view.

I force my legs to move, and when Chase comes running into the room to show me the paper airplane he just made, I draw the blinds. My five-year-old is not ready for that view, nor am I ready for that conversation.

"Daddy, look what Emma showed me how to make."

He throws it and it crashes to the bed. He dives for it, picks it up and flies it out of the room. I grin as I watch him go. Where the hell does he get all the energy? Doors slam in the driveway next to mine, and little Sophie's voice can be heard in the cul-de-sac as she rushes into her house. I guess the Castellos are home. Not that it's any of my business, but I might wander over, find out if Anna is the new nanny, or maybe she's a long-lost relative they forgot to mention.

Is that really why you want to go over, dude?

Okay fine. Maybe I'm man enough to admit that I might like another sneak peek, might like to feel her silky skin against mine. Christ, our hands barely touched at the grocery store, and here I am getting a boner as I call on the memory. Seriously though, I might not be the best judge of character when it comes to women, but Anna is far too young for me—far too innocent—and I'm not interested in a relationship with anyone, anyway. Not after Chase's mother said she didn't want the responsibility that came with a child. Then she up and left with half of what was in my savings account, leaving me to care for our son alone. Throw in the law firm I own, and the conferences I must attend, and I can barely keep my head above water. Don't even get me started on how many nannies we've been through. I have rules in place for a reason. If they can't follow them, they know where the door is.

I shrug out of my suit jacket and loosen my tie. Unable to help myself, I lift the blinds and disappointment gathers in my gut when I find the neighbor's pool empty. Did I really think she was going to hang around to give me another show? No, but a guy can hope. I snort as I shed my work clothes and pull on a T-shirt and pair of shorts. It's been a long time since I've been with someone, but messing around with the neighbor's young nanny is not in my best interest.

I head downstairs, and Emma smiles up at me from the kitchen table. She's young, about twenty, but so far, she seems to be working out just fine. She's lasted a whole month, and I have high hopes.

"Why don't you take the rest of the day off, Emma? After a week alone with Chase, I'm sure you could use a break." Her smile wavers, like she fears I'm testing her. "Go," I say. "Go have some fun with your friends."

"Thank you, Mr. Hail," she says, and I shake my head. Christ, I'm thirty-two, not that much older than her, but she refuses to call me Alek. My last name isn't really Hail either. It's short for Mikhail, but I changed it up for a reason. As I think about that reason, my stomach knots. Christ, I love my parents. They spent their whole life caring for me, and while I might not have joined the family business, and they gave me their blessing to find my own way in life, I still feel like I'm letting them down.

They've always wanted to see me married and settled. Now that my ex is gone and I'm a single dad, they're pushing for marriage, insisting Chase needs a mother. They're not wrong. He does need a mother, but I'm not interested in an arranged marriage. As far as I'm concerned, there are two types of women in this world—those who run the other way when they find out where I come from, and those who want to get into my good graces because they want stature and money when they find out where I come from. I'm not interested in either. That's still not stopping my folks from pressuring me, and I have a shit ton of guilt over it.

Emma leaves the room, and I glance at Chase. "You really like Emma, huh?"

"I do." He flies his plane around the room, and my heart pinches. He's been through a lot, too much for a five-year-old. What kind of person just walks out on their child?

"Want to go see Sophie?"

"Yes. I want to show her my airplane."

I scruff up his hair with my hands. "Maybe she'd like to join us for some chicken nuggets."

His eyes go wide. "Is it Friday?" he asks.

I laugh. "No, it's not, but I've been away all week, and you were so good for Emma, I thought you deserved some chicken nuggets."

He throws his arms around my waist. "I missed you, Daddy. You were gone sooooo long."

Guilt races through my blood, his words hurting my heart. "I know, bud, but I shouldn't have to go away for a very long time now. Come on, let's go see what Sophie is up to."

"Me and Sophie went swimming at her pool, and then my pool. Emma got us ice cream, and Sophie dripped hers all over her bathing suit. Anna had to get her a clean one before she went back in the pool." Talking a mile a minute, he rushes down the hall, beating me to the front door.

I perk up when he mentions Anna. "Who's Anna?" I ask. Jesus, what have I become? I'm questioning my five-year-old now.

"She's Sophie's nanny. I like her."

I like her too.

He runs ahead, down our winding walkway, all the while flying his plane. "What do you like about her?"

"She played Marco Polo with me." I hurry to catch up with him and note his frown.

"What's up, little man?"

"She got real scared when the wind blew the door closed and it made a big bang."

"I guess it was loud, huh?" And that Anna spooks easily.

He covers his ears. "Really loud."

"Did it scare you?"

He lifts his chin an inch. "I'm not afraid of the wind."

I fight off a chuckle as we reach the neighbor's driveway. He picks up his speed and runs to the door, and by the time I get there, Chase is already running through their house in search of Sophie, and I stand there for a moment, taking in Anna's big blue eyes, and the way her mouth is gaping.

"You," she says, her gaze moving past me. She looks at my house. "It *was* you," she says, her voice a breathless whisper as she continues to stare at me, and I try not to gawk at her lush cleavage, tucked inside a pink, frilly, sleeveless blouse. Fuck, man, she can't be this innocent. She just can't be. Unless she'd been sheltered her entire life. "You...live there?" Her hand lifts, one shaky finger aimed at my place.

"Yeah. What a coincidence, huh?" Once again, I remind myself, in my world, coincidences don't exist. Every move is calculated, and with purpose.

I hold my hand out. "I guess if we're neighbors, an official introduction is in order, don't you think? I'm Alek."

I take her hand in mine, swallowing it whole, and I'm not one-hundred percent sure, but I think I just heard a small gasp catch in her throat.

"Anna," she whispers.

"I know, you told me already."

She shakes her head. "Right. Mr..."

"It's just Alek," I tease, although there is a part of me that wants her to call me Mr. Hail...in the bedroom.

Fuck me.

"Um, okay. Alek, it's nice to meet you." She blinks rapidly, and jerks her thumb over her shoulder. "Um, about the pool—"

I hold both of my hands up, palms out. "It's not what you think."

"What do I think?"

"I wasn't watching you. I just happened to glance out the window, and you were there."

Her face pales slightly. "Did you see..."

"I didn't see anything," I fib, and while we both know it's not the truth, we're both going to cling to that belief if that's what makes her sleep better at night. It's probably going to keep me up, in numerous ways.

"Thank God." She relaxes slightly, something about her innocence, her vulnerability, fucks with me in the worst ways. Christ, it's all I can do not to bundle her in my arms and take her home with me—protect her from the world. But if I had her home with me, I'm the one she'd need protection from. "I wouldn't want Mrs. Castello to think I flashed you. I *need* this job."

My gaze moves over her pretty face, the worry lingering in the depths of her blue eyes. "I don't think she'd fire you over an accident."

She shrugs. "I'm new. I really want to make a good impression."

She sure made a good impression with me.

"I'm sure they love you." I lean into her. "The popsicles were a big hit. Thank you."

She smiles, but it falls quickly, and her eyes go big. "I'm sorry. I didn't even invite you in." She backs away and waves her hand. "Mr. and Mrs. Castello are both out at the pool with Sophie. I assume you know the way."

"I do." I step inside, and head toward the back of the house, and her quick footsteps sound on the marble floor behind me. I head out back into the sunshine and find Chase flying his plane, and Sophie chasing him.

Gio jumps up. "Alek, how was Atlanta?"

"Hot," I say and he laughs.

He gestures to a chair. "Let me get you a cold drink." I glance at Theresa, who is smiling at me. "How are you, Theresa?"

"Better now that you're here," she says graciously and flirtatiously as I take her hand in mine and kiss it.

"Theresa, could you at least wait until I'm no longer in earshot before you start flirting with our neighbor," Gio barks, feigning hurt.

We all laugh at that, and Theresa waves a dismissive hand his way, but Gio has nothing to worry about. The two of them are totally in love, and in a way, I'm envious of what they have.

"Come sit next to me," Theresa says, and pats the lounge chair next to her. I'm about to drop into it when I notice a movement by the window. I glance up in time to see Anna. She jerks back quickly, and I bite back a grin. Was she trying to listen in? "Tell me everything that has been going on in your life. Have you found yourself a good woman yet?"

"You know I'm not looking."

"Leave the man alone," Gio says as he hands me a scotch and soda. I take a big drink and stretch out on the chair.

"I see you've hired some help." I jerk my head toward the door I came out of. "I actually met Anna at the grocery store earlier."

Theresa's eyes light up. "She's lovely, yes?"

I laugh. "Yes, she is lovely."

"Sadly, she's only eighteen. Too young for you, Alek."

"Agreed." I take another fast drink as Anna steps outside. My gaze rakes over her appreciatively as she picks Sophie's ladybug towel up off the ground and hangs it over the rail.

She checks on the kids, who are now playing in the treehouse, and smiles at Theresa when she walks back to us. "Dinner will be ready in thirty minutes."

"Can we set another place for Alek and Chase?" Theresa's hand falls open as she turns to me. "Alek you will stay, won't you?"

"I was actually going to ask you if Sophie could join Chase and me for chicken nuggets. I wanted to take him out to make up for being away."

"You are such a good father." She shakes her head, and I don't need to ask to know she's thinking about Chase's mother. "I'm sure Sophie would love to go. But would you mind if Anna joined you all as well?"

"Oh...I..." Anna fumbles backward as she stumbles over her words.

"Would you mind, Anna? I think it's important for you and Sophie to spend some quality time together outside the house."

I arch my brow and eye Theresa, giving her the look. The one that says she'd better not be matchmaking. Then again, maybe she's not. She just finished telling me Anna was too young for me. Maybe she's trying to pull some kind of reverse psychology shit on me.

Theresa leans into me, her eyes serious. "It's important they bond this first week. Sophie needs special attention, you know."

I nod. Okay, I guess she's not trying to matchmake. "We'd love to have Anna join us." Even though I don't really know much about communication disorders in children, but if she says they need to stick together, then I'm in total agreement. "How does that sound to you, Anna? Would you like to come with us?" I grin at her. "Don't worry, we have more than chicken nuggets."

"Yes, of course," she agrees, just like I knew she would. She needs this job and is doing her damndest to be obliging. It's a good goddamn thing she's not my nanny, though. A real good goddamn thing, because if she was, I might want to push her a little, to see how innocent she really is, and discover just how far she'd go to please me.

3

ANNA

The house is dark, silent, and I stare at the ceiling, my mind racing a million miles an hour. I didn't want to go out to dinner with Alek tonight, didn't want to sit across from him at a fancy restaurant, our knees brushing under the table. No, I didn't want that at all, it was torturous and...arousing. But do you know what I really and truly didn't want? I didn't want to like the way the big commanding man made me feel safe and secure. I'm none of those things, not while I'm in hiding, and I know better than to rely on a man to protect me.

God, I've spent my whole life around powerful, dangerous men like Alek. But those men always made me feel small, controlled, a mafia princess that should be seen, not heard. Alek, however, his mere presence, his authoritative nature, hit me a little differently, and tugged at a need deep inside me, a need to be touched, kissed...held. I'm a virgin, but that doesn't mean I've never touched myself, never found pleasure with my own hand. Especially right now, as my hand creeps downward, dipping into my panties as my eyes slip shut, I visualize a very different finger touching me, stroking deep between my legs.

I slide my finger over my slick clit, and bite back a moan. The last thing I want is to wake the household, and have Theresa, Gio or both come running in to check on me. I realize what I do in my own bedroom is my own business, but I don't want to do anything that might put my job at risk—and that includes fantasizing about the hot daddy next door.

I can't lose sight of my goal. Work long enough to get enough cash that I can get out of Chicago and make it on my own. I suck in a breath as my finger slicks over my damp sex. I rub myself until my body is vibrating with need. Seconds before a shuddering climax overtakes me, a loud bang outside reverberates through me, and my gasp of need turns to a gasp of fear.

I remove my hand from my panties, my breathing fast as I sit up, and brace my feet on the floor, fight or flight instincts kicking in. Is there someone outside? One of my father's men, perhaps? I push from the mattress, and quietly tiptoe to the window to glance out. The pool area is quiet, but someone could be lurking in the bushes. I scan the grounds, and from my peripheral vision, catch movement in Alek's backyard. Surely to God, he's not awake and walking around his yard at two in the morning. Is there an intruder?

Then again, maybe he can't sleep either. Maybe he's over there, thinking about my hands on his body, the way I'm over here thinking about his on mine. I might be young and innocent, but I've been around enough men in my life to know they look at me like I'm a fresh piece of meat. A shiver wracks my body as I think about the creep that cornered me once in the upstairs hallway of my childhood home. One of Dad's top security guards caught him. I quiver to think what might have happened if Antonio hadn't come along. I never set eyes on that creep again and never asked what happened to him.

I nearly lost my bathing suit top in front of Alek today, and as much as I was worried about losing my job, I have to admit, I kind of liked his eyes on me. What the hell is it about him that is messing with my mind and body? I don't know, but I can only hope he stays on his side of the fence.

I'm about to head back to my bed when a bang, what sounds like a fence latch slamming shut, cuts through my thoughts. I grip my window and slide it up. The cooler night air washes over my near naked body as I stick my head out.

I narrow my eyes, try to see in the dark. Someone or something is creeping in Alek's back yard. Should I go over there or call the police? No, I can't have the police snooping around, and possibly identifying me. A beam of light illuminates Alek's backyard, and my heart jumps into my throat at the sight of him standing by his pool, dressed only in his swim shorts, staring up at me.

I jerk back, and groan as I press my back to the wall. My room is dark. There's no way he could have seen me, right? I take a few deep breaths and don't dare move. I'll wait it out, wait until he turns his light off and goes back into his house. A good two minutes pass and I let loose a relieved breath, sure he hadn't seem me.

"Hey," I hear from below.

Oh, hell no.

I stop breathing, hoping he'll just go away.

"If you don't come down here, then I'm coming up."

Oh, shit.

I tentatively push off the wall, and move in front of the window. "What...what are you doing here, Alek?"

"I want to know why you were watching me."

Oh God. I try to steady my breathing, when I say, "I wasn't. I heard a noise, and it scared me. I just came to see if there was someone in the yard."

"Why would someone be in the yard at two in the morning?"

"You tell me. You're the one in the yard at two in the morning."

He goes quiet, so quiet I wonder if I'm sleeping, and this is just a dream.

"Come on down," he says, his voice a low soft command. It sends shivers skittering through my body.

"No, I...I can't."

"I wasn't asking, Anna."

I grip the windowsill, my pulse thumping in my neck. "What do you want, Alek?"

"I can't sleep. You obviously can't sleep. Maybe a good hard swim will help us both."

A good hard something might help you, Anna.

Omg, where did that come from?

"I..." I glance over my shoulder, like a kid about to get caught with their hand in the cookie jar. I'm not a kid, though. I'm an eighteen-year-old woman, and is there anything wrong with me going for a swim with my hot neighbor?

Yes, everything.

I stare down at him, and everything in my gut tells me if I don't go down, he'll come up. I got to know him a bit over dinner, and while he was so good with the kids, it's easy to tell he's not a man people say no to.

"Give me a second to change."

I back away from the window, pull on a pair of shorts and a T-shirt, and quietly open my bedroom door. I tiptoe through the hall, hurry down the stairs and make my way to the back deck. My heart does an excited little thump when I find Alek standing there waiting for me. God, I shouldn't be doing this.

He doesn't say a word. Instead, he swallows up my hand with his, and guides me to his backyard. I let him lead me and try not to stare at the muscles on his back as they tighten and bunch with each movement. I've been around half-dressed boys before, at the country club pool, but Alek is far from a boy, and for some reason his attention excites me.

Once we're away from the house, he turns to me, and his gaze rakes over my clothes. "That's what you're wearing to go swimming?"

"I wasn't planning on swimming." I glance at his big pool, much like the Castellos, like the one I grew up with, and plunk myself down on a plush lounge chair. Earlier tonight, I thought we'd be going to some fast-food restaurant for chicken nuggets, but he took us all to an expensive restaurant that prepared chicken nuggets for the kids even though it wasn't on the menu. This man obviously has a lot of pull.

"Who are you?" he asks, his question taking me by surprise.

"I'm Anna. Who are you?"

He drops down into a chair next to me. "You know what I mean."

"I'm Anna, nanny for your neighbors."

He stares at me, and I'm so aware of his hot, hard body, his close presence, it's hard to draw in air. "Tonight, at dinner, you looked spooked."

"I don't eat out a lot. It was a big restaurant." It's not a lie. I've been so damn sheltered, and we have an excellent cook at home who taught me so much.

"Why did you think there was someone in your backyard?"

"Because there was," I shoot back.

A small smile curls his lips, and my brain stops firing. Does he have any idea how good looking he is? He doesn't have a ring on his finger, and I don't think he's married—not anymore. Still, I shouldn't be out here with him.

He leans toward me, and I instantly lean back. He scrubs his chin, his hot gaze moving over my face. "Are you afraid of me, Anna?"

"I don't know you."

"It's probably better that way," he whispers so quietly, I'm not even sure I heard him right. He stands and turns his back to me. Without a word, he walks to his pool and dives in. With my insides quivering, I push to my feet and walk to the edge. A second later he surfaces, and his hands go to my ankles. His fingers are cold, yet they still manage to send heat straight to my core.

"Are you coming in?" he asks.

Heat burns through me, but I'm pretty sure not even the cool water will help tamp it down. He lets go of my legs and swims away, giving me room to dive in. I don't dive. Instead, I jump, staying close to the edge, as far away from Alek as possible. I surface and he's right there, so close, I can feel his warm breath on my cheek.

"I'll find out, you know."

I take in the concern on his face and ask, "Find out what?"

"Find out who you are, and what you're running from."

"I'm not running from anyone," I lie and push away, swimming to the middle of the pool. He follows me, and we tread water.

"Are you in trouble, Anna? If you are, I—"

"I'm not," I say quickly, too quickly, judging by the way he's staring at me, his head angled like I'm a puzzle he can't quite figure out. "I'm nobody to waste your time over." Switching subjects, I ask. "What do you do, Alek? You must be someone very important to have a gorgeous mansion like this."

Eyes dark, he backs up. His muscles grow tight, as he goes to the side of the pool, climbs out and sits on the edge. "I'm a lawyer."

I nod. Lawyers can make good money, but this guy is loaded, and his body language tells me one thing: he doesn't want me to know who he is any more than I want him to know who I am.

A light flicks on upstairs, and I spin. "I think we might have woken someone."

"That's Emma's room, and she knows the rules."

"Rules."

"When I'm out here at night, the backyard is off limits. Her blinds stay shut."

"If they don't?"

"I fire her."

"Brutal."

"My rules are meant to be followed, Anna."

"You come out at night a lot."

"It's when I do my best thinking."

"What did you need to think about tonight?" I ask, and he draws in a very deep breath, his gaze so intense, so focused on me, I can't help but wonder if I'm the reason he couldn't sleep.

I swim to the stairs, and wring my T-shirt out as I climb the steps, cursing myself for not putting on a bra. I really wasn't expecting to swim, and my nipples are granite hard. Not just from the water or the cooler night air rushing over my flesh.

I lift my head, and Alek is right there. His big hands span my waist, and he carefully lifts me from the last step, placing me directly in front of him. Big, protective hands stay on my waist, providing a measure of comfort, security, and warmth I'm not accustomed to. Dark eyes drop, taking in my hard nipples, and he doesn't even try to hide the fact that he's checking me out, or taking pleasure in my tight buds.

He takes a step closer to me, and a sound catches in my throat as his erection presses against my stomach. He's rock hard. A thrill I shouldn't feel burns through me, pushing back the cold.

His fingers widen, and without permission, he lightly caresses my nipples. He groans, like he's in total agony, and his erection presses harder against my body.

He cups my chin, lifts it until I'm staring into his dark eyes. My heart crashes against my ribs, as need and want careen through my body. I shift restlessly, arch into him, wanting more attention on my nipples. Never in my life have I been so brazen, felt so sure of something or someone. I honestly have no idea what is going on with me, and when his deep, throaty groan curls around me, I don't really care.

"Alek," I say, a pleading tone to my voice. I want him to kiss me, to toss me onto the lounge chair and have his way with me. Not just because it will de-value me and make me a less attractive match for a rival family, but because I want to feel this man inside me.

"What do you want, Anna?"

"I...you."

A dog barks in the distance, the sound cutting through the stillness of the night. He straightens to his full height, a noticeable shift in him. His body tightens, all lust gone from his eyes.

"You should go."

My stomach drops, and I stand there blinking up at him, positive I didn't hear him right.

"Alek?"

"You should go," he says again, his artic cold voice turning my blood to ice.

His words hit like a slap to the face, and I take a small step back. God, I am so stupid. I hate myself for wanting a man who could so easily discard me. He's no different than any other man in my life, and I'd be wise to remember that.

"You were the one who brought me here," I shoot back, my hard, cold tone matching his eyes. Was this just a game to him? Does he get his kicks playing with innocent girls, teasing and torturing their arousal, and tossing them away once he gets them to submit to his needs? But he was hard too. He wanted this. Maybe he realizes just how inexperienced I am and doesn't think I can please him.

The muscles in his jaw clench. "It was a mistake."

He backs up, leaving cold where there was once heat, leaving vulnerability where there was once safety. Tears pound behind my eyes, but I refuse to cry. This cruel man doesn't deserve my tears. But what he does deserve, is a good hard—torturous—look at what he could have had.

It's on, neighbor.

ALEK

What the fuck was I thinking?

I walk around my office, the staff steering clear of me as they have been all day, my mood as dark as the heavy rain clouds threating to rip open outside. I shouldn't have gone to the neighbor's house last night. Shouldn't have insisted—ordered—Anna to come downstairs. And I really shouldn't have taken her in my arms, brushed her nipples with my thumbs, or pressed my rock-hard cock against her soft lush body.

She's sweet and innocent and the last thing she needs is to be mixed up in my dangerous family. Besides that, I'm sure she's running or hiding from something. I'll be damned if that doesn't bring out the protector in me and while I know it's in my best interests to keep a measure of distance from her, how can I when I know she could be in some kind of trouble? Talk about a rock and a hard place and yes, the hard place is between my legs.

Thank God for the reprieve of my office. No way could I be at home, knowing she was next door, or possibly seeing her at the pool again, in that ridiculously too big bathing suit that exposed her gorgeous body, or those sexy shorts and T-shirt she was in last night. Fucking hot. I abused myself a couple of times before I fell into a restless sleep.

My phone buzzes and I ignore it. I'm not in the mood to talk to anyone right now. I open my laptop, and check emails, all the while trying to ignore my phone.

My assistant pokes her head in. "Mr. Hail."

"What?" I lash out, and shake my head when she flinches. Shit, I'm not upset with her. I'm upset with myself and the situation I suddenly find myself in. I shouldn't be biting her head off. "I'm sorry, Nancy. Just some things on my mind. What is it?"

"It's Emma." She nods toward my ringing phone. "She needs to speak to you."

My stomach tightens, and I snatch the phone off the cradle. "Emma," I say. "Is Chase okay?"

"He's fine," she says quickly. "He's perfectly fine, Mr. Hail."

I let loose a relieved breath. "What is it then?"

"I...uh..." She hesitates for a second, and I frown. She knows I don't like hesitancy. If she has something to say, she just needs to say it. Maybe she's worried it will upset me.

"Emma?"

"I can no longer work for you, Mr. Hail."

Shit. I sit up a bit straighter. "Is there a problem? I thought things were working out."

"Yes...no...I'm taking another job."

No. No. No. This can't be happening. She was working out so well. Okay, you got this, Alek, change her mind. I call on my negotiation skills. "If this is about compensation, I can—"

"It's not."

"Is it the rules?" They're in place for a reason, but I suppose I could relax some if it meant keeping her. The thoughts of going back to the agency again, interviewing and firing again...Jesus, I don't have time for this.

"No, I just have to go. You're going to have to come home, or maybe I can see if Anna can watch Chase until you get off work. I need to go right now."

I shake my head, trying to wrap my brain around the urgency in her voice, and her sudden need to leave. Things were going so well. What the fuck is going on?

"I'm on my way. Don't leave," I command. "I want you to keep Chase with you until I get there." I'm dealing with enough as it is. The last thing I need is to see Anna, and remember how her lush breasts felt beneath my fingertips. I slam the phone down, snatch up my briefcase and head toward the door.

"I have to leave. Forward all calls to my place," I say as I rush to leave.

Nancy gives me a curt no-nonsense nod. "Will do, Mr. Hail."

Outside I jump into my car, maneuver through busy afternoon traffic, and arrive home much later than I would have hoped. The house is quiet, locked up. Is she gone? Goddammit, I asked her to stay. Okay, maybe ordered is the better word. I guess she no longer has to follow any of my rules, if she's quitting.

I hurry up the walkway, and voices reach my ears. I stop, turn and follow the path to the backyard. At the fence, I spot Anna, Sophie, and Chase in the water. Emma is sitting in a lounge chair, her legs shaking in a nervous manner as she checks her phone. I open the fence and all eyes turn to me as it creaks.

Emma jumps to her feet, and I notice her luggage at her side. Before I can ask what's really going on, Chase jumps from the pool and comes running over. He throws his wet arms around my body, and I sink down to hug him.

"Hey little man, are you having fun?"

He frowns. "No, Emma is leaving."

I nod, and run my hand over his hair, as my gaze slides to the pool, to Anna, who is bouncing around in the water with Sophie. I try not to stare at her tits; now is not the time for a hard on. I'm in the middle of a goddamn crisis.

"Why don't you go play and I'll talk to Emma. Afterward, we'll all have popsicles."

He nods, and jumps back into the pool, water splashing over my suit. "Can we talk?" I say to Emma as she stands there shifting from one foot to the other.

"Sorry, Mr. Hail. No time. I have to leave right now."

I eye her, trying to figure out if someone in my family got to her. But what would be the purpose? My parents love Chase, and they know he needs a caretaker when I'm at work. They'd have no reason to push Emma out of our lives.

"Is it about the rules?"

She shakes her head, and a car horn sounds in the driveway. "That's my uber. I'm sorry to leave so suddenly. But there is a family that needs me right away."

"I need you, Emma. Chase needs you. I'll triple whatever the other family is paying you."

She hesitates for a brief second and closes her eyes. When she opens them again, there's fierce determination there. "Sorry, I have to go."

I stand there dumbfounded as she walks away, and after she disappears around the corner, I drop down onto a lounge chair and tug at my tie. I brace my elbows on my knees and drop my head into my hands.

"Are you okay?" Anna asks, her voice breaking into my thoughts.

I lift my head and wish I hadn't. She's in that ridiculously loose bathing suit again. If she moves the wrong way, her nipple is going to pop out. She pulls a chair up and sits across from me, and I try not to stare at her half naked body, try not to visualize how she'd look in my bed, my cock buried deep inside her.

Fuck me.

"Do you know why she left?"

"Sorry, I don't." She glances over her shoulder, as Sophie and Chase sit at the edge of the pool, eating watermelon. "I can try to help out with Chase until you find someone new."

I shake my head. "Thanks, but you're Sophie's nanny, not mine. She needs one on one attention, and I don't want you to split your focus. I'll call the agency."

"Okay, but I'm here if you need me."

Fuck, she has no idea what I need, and if she did, she wouldn't be putting any kind of offer on the table.

She puts her hands on her knees, and inches them open ever so slightly.

I nearly bite off my tongue. What the ever-loving fuck is she doing? My cock thickens, as I imagine myself between those legs, shoving that skim of material to the side and running my tongue all over her damp sex. I take a breath. I suppose I deserve this kind of teasing. I did, after all, nearly fuck her, and then put an abrupt stop to it.

"Chase, come on inside," I grumble, needing to tear myself away before I do something I will only regret later.

"I want to play with Sophie," he yells back.

I'm about to protest, but Anna's hand lands on my knee. "You go ahead and make some calls. We're all okay out here. I'll get everyone a popsicle."

My dick thickens from her touch, and a groan I have no control over crawls out of my throat as I imagine her sucking on that popsicle...my dick. Jesus, I should just fuck her.

No, no you shouldn't, dude.

"Okay. They're in the freezer."

"Of course, they are. Where else would they be?"

"Yeah..."

She jumps up, heads into the house, and comes back with popsicles. The kids stand and run off to the playhouse, and Anna walks toward them. She bends, offering me a gorgeous view of her ass, as she picks up a few towels. She straightens and my gaze follows her sweet ass as she saunters off, and I can't help but think that extra sway to her hips is on purpose. I'm pretty sure the hot nanny next door is trying to make me lose it. Christ, the last thing she wants is to unleash my tether and set me free on her.

She hands the popsicles out, and sits at the picnic table beside the playhouse and runs her tongue over hers. That's my cue to get the fuck out of here.

I stand and call out to Chase. "Be good for Anna. I have a few calls to make."

I head inside and adjust my dick in my pants. The first thing I do is go to my room, kick off my shoes and socks and change into something more comfortable. Once I'm changed, I make my way to my home office, and take a look out the window. I spot Anna bent over, her sweet ass aimed my way. Jesus, the things I'd like to do to that ass.

Without thinking, I slide my hand into my shorts and take my dick into my palm, and the second I do, Anna stands and turns my way, like she can feel my eyes drilling into her. Her gaze holds mine, and I stroke myself, once, twice and when a small grin curls up her lips, I curse under my breath and pull my hand from my pants.

What the fuck is it about her that's reducing me to a hormonal teenager? I'm a grown man for fuck's sake. If I want to fuck, I can go find someone to fuck.

But you want Anna.

I push away from the window. I have no idea what kind of game we're playing. But watching each other through the glass has to stop, although really, I was the one who started it. With my attention finally focused on the task at hand, I call the agency. I ask about Emma, and if they suddenly had to place her elsewhere and a knot forms in my stomach when I'm told they have no idea what I'm talking about. I am pleased however, to hear they'll send someone by right away for an interview.

I end the call, walk to the kitchen and take out a soda. I stare at the fridge for another second and grab one for Anna. Outside I find her sitting on the edge of the pool as the two kids color at the table.

"Drink?" I ask.

She glances up at me with those light blue eyes of hers. "Thanks."

I twist the lid and hand her the bottle. She takes a big gulp, and the second her tongue snakes out to swipe her bottom lip, I know I'm screwed, because yeah, I'm going to have to fuck her.

I'm about to head back inside, but she taps the empty spot beside her. "Have a seat."

Probably not a good idea. I drop down beside her. My feet dangle in the cool water, and I must admit, it is refreshing.

"Any luck?" she asks.

"The agency is sending someone over this afternoon."

She nods. "That's good to hear. I'm sure she'll be perfect."

My gaze rakes over the beautiful girl beside me. She's so damn hot, lush and tempting.

She's only eighteen, dude.

Old enough to consent.

As I shut down those dueling voices, I say, "Yeah, perfect."

"I suppose I should get Sophie back home. I have to prepare dinner." She stands up, and goddammit, she is the perfect height. With her standing, and me sitting her pussy is right there, inches from my mouth. It's all I can do not to grab her by the hips, pull her against my face, and feast.

"Anna, Sophie," Theresa calls out from the other side of the fence, and I quickly pull myself together.

I stand and pray to fuck no one can see my thickening cock. "Come on in, Theresa."

She opens the latch and saunters over, her arms filled with designer bags, and while she's smiling, there's a nervousness about her, an edge I haven't seen before.

"Everything okay?"

"Delightful," she answers. "I did a bit of shopping after my meeting with the school board. It's hard to believe Sophie starts classes in a couple weeks. Chase too." Sophie runs to her mom and hugs her legs. "Darling, are you having the best time?"

"Il...meglio," Sophie answers in Italian, a language that comes more naturally to her than English.

Anna gathers up their towels and squeezes the water from her hair. "I was just on my way over to get dinner started."

Theresa waves a dismissive hand. "No need, tonight we will be ordering in. We have much to discuss after my meetings."

Anna nods. "Oh, okay."

"You'll be joining us of course, Alek," Theresa says with a smile. "My cousin Maria is coming for a visit. She's a lovely girl."

Christ, no more matchmaking and while I'd like to say no, I am curious. How did her meeting go, and what is it she has to discuss with Anna? "I don't think I can. The agency is sending over a nanny for me to interview."

"Oh yes," she says, not at all surprised.

I narrow my eyes. "You knew Emma was leaving?"

Her eyes go wide. "No, no of course not. That is horrible news, Alek." She places a hand on my arm, her diamonds glistening in the late day sun. "What happened?"

"I'm still trying to figure that out myself." I snap my fingers. "She just up and left basically."

"Terrible to get good help these days. I lucked out with Anna...but..."

"But what."

"Tonight. Dinner. Come after the interview. We will wait for you, and I am not taking no for an answer."

I glance at my watch. "They did say they would send someone right away."

"It's settled then." She takes Sophie's hand and Anna follows them out. "We'll see you soon," Theresa calls over her shoulder.

They disappear, and I turn to Chase. "Come on, bud. Let's go get cleaned up."

"Daddy, I miss Emma."

"I know, me too."

He glances up at me with those big hopeful eyes. "Can Anna be my nanny? I like Anna."

"Sorry, bud, she's Sophie's nanny." He frowns, and it's ridiculous how much I hate disappointing him. I scoop him up. "We'll find someone awesome, okay?"

He puts his arms around my neck. "Okay, Daddy."

We head inside, and after we both change into nice clothes for dinner, the doorbell rings. I take Chase's hand, and we open the door to find an elderly woman standing on my stoop. She has a scowl on her face, and Chase inches backward, hiding himself behind my legs.

"I'm Hilda. From the agency."

"Yes, come in please."

She grumbles something under her breath, and I can't help but think whoever sent her here had gone mad. Then again, maybe she's a lovely woman once you get to know her. I gesture for her to sit on the sofa, and Chase sticks close.

"What experience do you have?" I ask.

She lifts her head and hands me a resume. "Thirty long years in the business."

I glance at her resume. "Very impressive."

"I can start first thing tomorrow but you must know, I don't tolerate temper tantrums, and I run a tight ship. Rules need to be followed."

"I see." Christ, is that what I sound like? An intimidating bastard? No wonder Emma left.

"Daddy..." Chase tugs on my shirt. "Daddy, can I go play Lego?" Clearly, he wants out of the room every bit as much as I do.

Hilda points a finger at him. "You should not interrupt like that, young man. No worries we'll fix that."

Okay, interview over.

I stand. "Thanks for stopping by, Hilda. I'll let the agency know of my decision."

"Don't wait too long. Nannies like me don't come by every day."

Thank God for that.

I guide her out and Chase looks terrified when I turn back to him. 'Don't worry, little buddy. We'll keep looking until we get someone we like." He lets out a relieved breath. "Want to head over to Sophie's for dinner?"

A smile lights up his face and warms my heart. Five minutes later, we're seated at the big dining room table, waiting for our food delivery. Gio fixes me a drink, and I don't miss the way Theresa's cousin Maria is staring at me. I shift, a bit uncomfortable as she looks at me like she wants to eat me alive. I wish Theresa would quit trying to set me up. At least she's not trying to match me with Anna. She wouldn't have brought Maria here if she was.

I take a big drink, and my gaze travels to Anna, who is talking to my son. My heart pinches tight. She's so good with the kids. But it wouldn't be a good idea for her to be my son's nanny. Not when all I can think about is stripping her bare and having my way with her. That certainly couldn't happen if I was her boss, right? A total conflict of interest, and the agency has strict policies about such things.

I don't miss the way Theresa makes eye contact with her husband, a sudden nervousness about her. I sit up a bit straighter everything in me warning that something bad is about to go down. I might not be a part of my family's dealings, but I was raised in a mafia family and can sense trouble miles away.

She clears her throat to get our attention. "I'm afraid I have some bad news," Theresa begins with a frown as she looks at Anna. "After talking to the school board, it has come to our attention that we have to hire someone with special needs training for Sophie. It's in her best interest. The agency found someone and will be sending them over. I'm so sorry about this, Anna. We loved having you in our home, and Sophie loves you too. But I'm sure the agency will be able to find you another position."

I glance at Anna, who has gone pale. Shit, she needs this job for reasons I don't know, but judging from the look on her face, it's clear the rug had just been pulled out from underneath her.

"Daddy, Daddy," Chase yells. "That means Anna can be my nanny now, right?"

"It does indeed, little man. It does indeed."

ANNA

I give a slow nod of my head, and put my hands flat on the table. For a second I think I'm going to fall off my chair, but I square my shoulders. "I understand. I want what is best for Sophie, too."

"I'm sorry to spring this on you," Theresa says, and my gaze slides to Alek. If she was going to fire me, did she have to do it in front of the neighbor and his son? Getting fired is mortifying enough, and now everyone is staring at me.

Keep it together, girl.

I push from the table and smooth my hand down my loose-fitting dress. Sophie is blinking up at me. We haven't been together for very long, but I've bonded with her. "Hey Sophie," I begin. "You're going to have a great new nanny and, you're going to have so much fun when you start school in a couple weeks." The room goes quiet as I bend to give her a hug, and she sits there struggling, like she can't find the right words, and she probably can't. And there is the reason she needs a nanny who can help her with her cognitive disabilities.

I turn to Chase, and ruffle his hair. "You watch out for Sophie at school, okay little man?"

"No," he blurts out.

"No, you won't watch out for Sophie?"

"You're not going anywhere, silly."

I drop to one knee. "Chase, I do have to go."

"No, you're going to be my nanny, right Daddy?"

All eyes turn to me, but I can only focus on Alek. His eyes narrow in on me and I can almost hear his brain racing, battling an internal war only he's aware of. But I think I get it. He doesn't want me under his roof. It probably wouldn't be in our best interests, especially after my display at his pool today. Aiming my ass right at him, just to show him what he could have had. What was I thinking? I don't know. I guess I felt foolish, rejected. Discarded. I never would have done any of that had I thought I'd be getting fired and he might be my next boss.

I briefly close my eyes, and imagine the hot daddy next door bossing me around. I gulp, because I like it, I like it a lot.

"Right, Daddy?" Chase asks again. "Anna can be my nanny."

I can hear Alek's throat as he swallows. I haven't known him long, but it's clear he has a hard time saying no to Chase. Would I say yes if he asked? I need to work if I want to get out of Chicago, but living in the same house as Alek would be hard.

You liked it when he got hard.

Oh, God.

"I didn't know you were looking for a nanny," Maria pipes up, reaching for Alek and putting her hand over his. She runs a long, manicured nail over his wrist. "I'm a great nanny. Tell him, Theresa. Tell him how great I am with kids."

"She's wonderful with kids," Theresa agrees.

"I want Anna," Chase blurts out, and you have to love a kid's honesty and lack of tact.

"I guess that settles it," Alek says, and my heart thumps in my chest. Theresa releases an audible sigh, and I glance at her. She quickly wipes the small smile from her face. "That is, if she's interested in the job."

I turn back to Alek, as Chase wiggles with delight in his seat. "I...I..."

"Is that a yes or no, Anna?" he asks, in a no-nonsense voice that shouldn't, but does ridiculous things to my insides.

"Do you really...want me?" His eyes darken as the words slip from my mouth. "I mean," I add quickly. "Don't feel pressured. I'm sure the agency can find me another placement."

"You're in need of a job. I'm in need of a nanny. It's a logical solution, wouldn't you say?"

Can't argue with that.

I nod, and he says, "Great. Do you need me to help you pack your things?"

"No," I quickly answer, my body so jittery I'm not sure how I'll be able to walk out of the room. "I don't have a lot." Just then the doorbell rings, and it snaps me back to attention. "The food has arrived. I'll get it." Before anyone can stop me,

I leave the dining room and dart down the hall. I fling open the door and the driver hands me numerous bags that I struggle to carry.

"Let me help."

Alek's deep voice comes from behind. Close enough that his breath warms my neck. A shiver travels down my spine, as he reaches around me to retrieve a few of the bags.

"Thanks," I say, and he uses his foot to shut the door when the delivery driver leaves. "Um, Alek…"

His head dips, his eyes dark and hungry when they land on me, and I wonder if it's me and not the food in our hands that's making him salivate. God, I never should have toyed with him this afternoon. Never should have showed him what he could have had. But now that I'm working for him, he can't have it, right? Which is good. I shouldn't be getting involved with him. It's not conducive to me making a clean break from Chicago.

"What is it, Anna?"

"Are you sure you want me to be your nanny?"

"You won't be my nanny, Anna. You'll be Chase's nanny."

A small laugh catches in my throat. "Yes, of course."

"I'll be your boss, and you'll be my employee."

"Right," I say. Okay, he's making this all about business. Good.

If it's so good, why is disappointment settling in your stomach?

"I'll call the agency to let them know. Right now, we should…" He gestures with a nod toward the dining room as delicious smells from the food reaches my nostrils.

"Right...food."

Alek inhales. "It smells amazing," he says about to carry the food to the dining room.

"Tastes even better."

He stops, and goes perfectly still, and that's when I realize what I'd said. Oh God, does he think I'm talking about me, and that I'd taste good. Maybe this is all in my head and there's nothing going on between us, and maybe he wasn't aroused and pressing his cock against me yesterday.

"I mean, the food. I've had it before. It's good. Really good."

"I knew what you mean," he murmurs through clenched teeth.

"We better get it divvied up before it gets cold."

I push past him and rush down the hall. Theresa is watching me carefully as I walk toward the dining room. I don't know her all that well, but she seems to be nervous about something. I guess she didn't like firing me any more than I liked getting fired. And now I'll be working for Alek. Ohmigod.

I open the bags and pull out the containers. Theresa opens them and we pass them around the table. I am quiet as we eat, and the conversation picks up around me. I don't pay close attention. How can I when I'm trying to figure out how I'm going to keep myself together when I'm living with Alek?

Once the meal is finished, Theresa sends me off to pack, and I dash upstairs to my room. I stand there for a long second, feeling a little lost inside, a little vulnerable, and maybe even a little afraid, when someone clears their throat at my door. I spin and find Alek standing there.

"Are you okay?" he asks, and without any kind of permission, he walks into my room.

Never forget he's the kind of man to take without asking, Anna.

"I...did you need something?" I ask and go to my closet to get my suitcase. Instead of answering, he takes my suitcase from me, opens it, and tosses it onto my bed.

"I can do this," I say and plant one hand on my hip.

"Get at it."

"I *was* getting at it. I only took a second to process getting fired. You don't have to stand over me."

"I'll stand over you if I want to stand over you. Now move it. Get your things so we can get home and get Chase settled for the night."

"You're not the boss of me," I mumble under my breath, sounding like a belligerent child being told what to do. Which is exactly what he's doing. I hate that I like it.

He steps up to me, his body close, his warm scent doing the most ridiculous things to my body. "The boss of you is exactly what I am, and I expect you to do as I say, and follow my rules. "

"Rules?"

"Yes, rules. We'll go over them tomorrow, and as long as you follow them, we'll get along just fine."

I take a few fast breaths as his head dips, his lips close to mine. Deep between my legs, my sex clenches, and I don't know what is going on with me. I hate pushy, bossy men. He's commanding and demanding, right up there with every other mafia henchman I've met.

What will he demand of me?

It's absolutely insane that I can't wait to find out.

"Right, boss." I salute him. "Should I call you Alek, or maybe boss man?" I eye him and tap my chin like I'm thinking it over. "No, no. You're the kind of guy who would prefer sir, right?"

His face goes hard, and his eyes blacken. As he looks down at me, all severe and intense, like he might slap my ass for talking back, I'm pretty sure I'm about to orgasm in my panties. Here I thought he couldn't be any hotter.

His jaw is tight when he says, "For now, you can call me Alek."

I nod. "Let's just go with sir," I say, liking the way it sounds on my tongue, and yeah, I can see what it's doing to him. He likes it. A lot. "Anna, at your service, sir."

"Now that that's settled." He steps around me, pulls the top drawer right out of my dresser, and dumps it into my suitcase. Heat crawls up my neck as he stands there for a moment, examining all my underwear. His hand snakes out and he takes one of my bikini tops in his hands. He rubs the fabric between his fingers, and my nipples go tight.

"First thing we'll be doing is getting you a bathing suit that fits." He turns to me. "Something your breasts don't spill out of." I gulp as his gaze drops and takes in my cleavage.

"I...I lost a bit of weight."

He eyes me, and I try not to squirm under his careful inspection. "Are you not eating?"

I glance down. "I'm eating." God, I can't tell him stress has been affecting my appetite. He might ask questions I can't—

won't—give answers to, and then I might be fired before I ever step foot in his place.

He puts his finger under my chin and lifts it until my eyes are on his. "You're not lying to me are you, Anna? One thing I can't tolerate is liars."

Must be the lawyer in him. Then again, I'm not a lawyer and I despise liars too. "Not lying."

"If I find you not eating. I'll sit you down and feed you myself. Chase is a handful. You need your strength, and I don't want you getting sick."

God, what is it about his take charge attitude that I love? I usually hate that in a man, but something about him wanting to take care of me, instead of dismissing me, tugs at a need deep inside me. "You don't have to take care of me."

He scrubs his face, an intensity about him that sparks something deep between my legs. "No?"

"No. I'm a big girl, and I can take care of myself. Besides, it's my job to take care of you and Chase."

He stares at me for a long time, and I work to control my breathing. When he finally steps away, and roughly pulls another drawer from the dresser, I dart into my bathroom to grab my toiletries, needing a quick moment to myself. My stupid hands are shaking as I gather up my things. Back in the bedroom, he's putting all the drawers back in place. I throw the rest of my things into my backpack, and he zips up my suitcase.

"Is that everything?" he asks. I nod, and give one last glance around my room. "Time to head next door and get you settled in my home."

Twenty minutes later, he's tossing my suitcase on a bed in his house, and I stand there and take in the room. It's nice, has its own bathroom, and is decorated in neutral shades of gray.

"This is your space. You can paint it if you like, and we can get new bedding if it suits you."

I sit on the bed, and test the mattress. "It's perfect." It's not like I'll be here for all that long. I just need to earn enough money to start a new life. I bounce up and down and a groan crawls out of Alek's throat.

"Stop doing that."

I instantly go still, and his gaze is latched on my breasts as they come to a rest. "Sorry, sir."

"Jesus," he murmurs, and walks to my door. His back muscles are tight, and I let my gaze fall, to take in his exquisite ass. "I'll see to getting Chase to bed tonight. You get yourself settled."

With that he closes my door, and I listen quietly to his footsteps descending the stairs. I jump from the bed, and go to the window to open it. My body is hot, and I need the breeze to help cool me down. I glance at the pool in Alek's backyard. His room must be right beside mine, judging by the way I can see into the neighbor's yard.

I unpack my things, and by the time I brush my teeth, change into a pair of pajama shorts and a T-shirt that are both a little too loose now, the house is quiet. I settle into my bed, but sleep just won't come. I toss on the comfy mattress, and kick off my blankets. I swallow against a dry throat and throw my feet over. I tip toe to my door, and press my ear against it. When I'm sure everyone is asleep, I go downstairs to get myself a big glass of water. On the counter beside the tap, I spot a jar, and note the little strips of paper in it. What the heck? Is that a to-do list or something? If so, he must be more regimented than I thought. I know he talked about rules, but this is insane, and maybe this won't work out between us at all.

But it has to, Anna. You must make this work.

I walk through the house. What happened to Chase's mother? I don't see any signs of a woman's touch, or any pictures. I take a drink of water, and head outside. The night air falls over me as I walk to the edge of the pool, and take a deep rejuvenating breath, mulling over the events of the day.

"What are you doing up?"

I shriek, spin, and lose my footing.

Oh, crap.

I jump from my chair so fast, I send it flying backward. Anna's scream curls around me as she windmills her arms and tries to stop herself from falling into the pool. I lunge for her, and she grabs my arm. Only problem is, we're both off balance, and I end up falling into the pool on top of her. She drops her glass into the water and as she sinks beneath my weight, I push myself upright, and reach down to fish her out.

She's sputtering and coughing by the time she surfaces, and my heart is crashing against my ribs worried I hurt her. I grip her shoulders. "Are you okay?"

"I...I..." She coughs some more, and I pick her up, and hurry to the stairs. I climb out and lay her flat out on the concrete decking.

I push her wet hair from her face. "Anna, can you breathe?"

Her eyes are big, frightened, and I tip her head back, about to perform CPR, when she coughs, and takes a big, deep breath. "I'm...okay," she says through fast heavy breaths. I try to quiet my racing heart as I keep a close eye on her. Once she's breathing regularly, I collapse beside her and stare at the star-studded sky, and try not to think about how bad this could have turned out.

"Were you trying to kill me?"

I go up on my elbow and roll onto my side. "No, of course not. Why would you ask that?"

"You were slinking around in the dark."

"Slinking? I wasn't slinking. I was sitting in that chair, having a drink."

"You waited until I was at the edge of the pool to say something."

"Not on purpose. I was just wondering what you were doing. I didn't mean to frighten you."

"It sure seemed like—"

Before she can get the words out, I lean over her and press my lips to hers. I don't know what's driving my actions. Maybe it's the adrenaline dump, or the thought of something bad happening to her. Her mouth is stiff at first, much like my cock when she first walked outside in next to nothing, the curve of her sweet ass cheeks taunting me in her too short pajama shorts.

Her lips soften against mine, and I grip her waist, hunger rising in me. I slide my hand higher, until I'm touching her outer breasts, and flick my thumb over her nipple, stiff from the cold water. Or maybe it's arousal. My cock thickens as my brain tells me to abort, but with the blood rapidly heading south, I'm afraid my cock is going to win this battle.

"What...are you doing?" she asks, as I kiss her.

"Mouth to mouth."

"Oh," she says, and slides her arms around me, accepting the ridiculous answer. The truth is, I'm fucking ravishing the hot nanny next door, who is now my son's nanny. Everything about this is wrong. She's too young, too lush, too fucking innocent for a guy like me.

She kisses me back, making me forget all the reasons I should jump in the pool again and cool myself off. I break the kiss, and press my lips to her throat, and her hips lift slightly.

"Have you fucked before, Anna?" I ask, and slide my hand down her flat stomach. I reach the band of her shorts and as everything inside me tells me to stop, I shove my hand inside. Her clit is wet and swollen, begging for attention as I brush my finger over it.

"Oh, God," she cries out.

"Answer me."

"Alek..." She lifts her hips again, and I run my finger around her tight opening.

Everything tells me she's a virgin, and I shouldn't be playing around with her like this. "Answer me."

"No," she says quietly. My hand stills, and I take a couple of fueling breaths to pull myself together. I need to get out of here. Now. I need to go to my room, and tug one out before I do something I can only regret later. I'm about to pull my hand out, but then she says, "No, I've never been fucked, sir."

"Sweet mother of God."

"What is it, sir?"

"Anna..." I warn. "You keep calling me that, and I'll fuck you hard. Right here. Right now."

I lift my head, and don't miss the heat in her eyes as her chest rises and falls rapidly. Jesus, I should leave well enough alone.

"If that's what you want, sir. I mean, you are my boss and I have to do what you want, right?"

I stare at her, take in the heat and need on her face. She stares back and I'm not even sure she's breathing.

"This afternoon, you were fucking with me, right? Trying to get my attention. Maybe even torture me a bit." She blinks up at me, a pretty shade of pink crawling up her neck. "I want the truth."

"Yes, sir. You see, I didn't like the way you worked me up and just dismissed me. I don't like being played with like that. I guess I thought I'd show you what you missed out on."

My brain spins, a war going on inside me. "You're a virgin."

"Yes."

"If you saved yourself this long, why do you suddenly want to be fucked?" She wiggles her hips, and my finger slips lower. I nearly lose all train of thought as my finger dips into her wet heat, and her sweet cunt clenches at the entrance. "Anna... you're so young."

"I'm of age and I'm consenting, sir."

Fuck me.

"Why me?" I ask. Why the hell would she pick me to give her virginity to?

"I like you," she says, but there's more. I can tell. There's more and she's not telling me, but I'll discover that later, but right now, she needs to be touched and I need to touch her.

"For the record, I like you too." I slide my finger inside her, going so deep a gasp rips from her mouth, and I nearly shoot off in my shorts. Tight. So goddamn tight, I'm going to ruin her with my cock and I can't fucking wait to do it. God, I can be a bastard.

I press my palm into her clit, and she moans. "Is this what you want? Me fucking you with my fingers?"

"And your cock."

Christ almighty. Maybe she's not so innocent, and maybe she's going to be the death of me. I pull my finger out and she whimpers.

"Alek, please..."

I climb over her, straddle her, and tug her until she's sitting. I grip the hem of her T-shirt and peel it over her head to expose her gorgeous breasts. "Fuck, Anna," I murmur as I take them in my hands. "How are you so perfect?"

"Because I'm untouched," she murmurs, and my cock nearly bursts from my shorts. I'm straddling a sweet little virgin who wants me to fuck her. I must have done something right in a past lifetime.

Too bad she's not going to get what she wants from me.

I find her mouth, kiss her deeply again as I savor the taste of her sweetness. My goddamn cock is straining so hard, it fucking hurts. I reach down, rip open my shorts, shove my boxers down, and free my cock. She gasps a little at the sound and pushes on my chest. For a second, I think she's having second thoughts, shoving me off her, but no, she just wants to see my cock. My throat tightens and goes dry. Sweet Jesus.

"You've never seen a cock, Anna?" Fuck, is that my voice?

"Yes. I mean, I do have the internet. But I've never seen a cock like yours." She reaches out, and tentatively touches the pre-cum dripping from my slit. She rubs it around before bringing her finger to her mouth for a taste, and I swear to God, I'm as good as dead here.

"Mmm," she says, and reaches for me again. I grip her wrist to stop her.

"No."

Dark lashes blink over confused eyes. "I did something wrong?"

"No, you did something right, but if you touch me again, I'm going to come."

She nibbles her lips, a look of pleasure dancing in her eyes. Sweet Anna likes fucking with me. I tear off my wet shirt and she examines my abs and chest as I put the material under her head and lay her back. As her tits beckon me, I reposition between her legs, and take her perfect pink nipple into my mouth. I suck hard, and she grips my hair and writhes beneath me.

"That's so good," she murmurs. I lick at her, swirl my tongue around her bud, and she makes gasping sounds. "I can feel it... between my legs."

Maybe I should have let her lie to me, tell me she's experienced. Her sweet innocence is a total mind-fuck. I shift off her body, and rub my cock on her leg as I dip back into her shorts. I inch a finger into her.

"Is this where you're feeling it?" I ask as I stroke the hot bundle of nerves inside her as I use the butt of my hand to stimulate her clit.

"Yes."

"Do you touch yourself, Anna? Do you use your hands or a toy?"

Something moves across her face. Something that looks like worry, distress. Was it something I said?

"My hand," She admits. "I don't have any toys."

"Would you like some toys?"

"I...don't know."

"There's a lot you don't know, isn't there?"

"Yes."

Fuck me, because man, I want to be the guy to show her everything, and I'm the last guy she should be messing around with. Despite that, I promise, "I'll show you everything."

Honestly, she's too innocent for the likes of my family, and while they want me to get married, for Chase to have a mother in his life, she has too much to do in life before she could step into that role. What the hell am I saying? I am not marrying this girl. No, I'm only giving her the sex she wants. And okay, yeah. I want it too.

I slide down, and grip her pajama bottoms. Her hips lift as I tug them down her legs. I do love the way she's helping me along. I grip her thighs, and spread them wide, putting her on display for me.

"So pretty," I say and pet her sex. I widen her damp pink lips, and lean in for a taste. Her moan mingles with mine as I slide my tongue along her silkiness.

"Alek, that feels so good." I take her clit into my mouth and twirl my tongue around it. "Ohmigod!"

I grin, loving her reactions. I apply more pressure, eat at her like a man starved and savor her sweet flavor on my tongue. She's soon writhing beneath me, her body craving release, and I push two fingers into her, widening and stretching her as I slide in and out.

Her breathing changes, becomes faster, erratic, and while I'd love to see her face when she comes, I'm too addicted to the taste of her to lift my head. Next time, when I have my cock in her, I'll see her face. Right now, she's so close, and there's nothing I want more than to give her a full body orgasm.

Her hands curl in my hair and she tugs as her sex muscles quiver around my finger. "Yeah, baby, come all over my mouth," I say.

"Alek…" Her whimpers curl around me, and the next thing I know, her body begins to spasm as she tumbles into a powerful orgasm. "That is…" She continues to clench around me, and I ease up on her sensitive clit and keep finger fucking her as she rides out the waves. I steal a fast glance up, and her head is tilted back, her eyes closed as she holds my face to her wet pussy.

My cock throbs, aching to be inside her, and I grit my teeth to keep myself from shooting off a load. Everything about the sight beneath me is mind-blowing. She chants my name under her breath, like she can't believe I just made her come. Her eyes inch open and a smile full of pleasure spreads across her face.

"Wow," she says, and I chuckle.

"Liked that huh?"

I crawl out from between her legs, and take my cock in my hand. She widens her legs, welcoming me, and it takes every ounce of strength I possess not to slam deep and take what I want. I bite down on my cheek and stroke myself. She sits up, blinks at me, her brow furrowed in confusion.

"Lay back, Anna," I demand in a soft voice.

She smiles and obliges, and instead of fucking her, I pump from base to crown.

"Aren't you going to fuck me?" she asks in a quiet voice.

"No."

"You don't want me?"

Fuck, she looks like she's about to cry. "Don't get me wrong here. I want to fuck you. I want to slide my cock into you and fuck you so hard you'll still feel me next week, but I'm not going to do that." My entire body stiffens, every muscle taught as I stroke myself. Christ, I want inside, but I can't rush this...can't rush her. She thinks she's ready, but she's not. "I mean, I am going to do that, Anna, but it won't be tonight. No, it will be when you're ready for me, and we have so much more experimenting to do before you're ready for my cock." There's understanding in her eyes as her gaze drops from mine and goes to my cock.

"Can I touch?"

"Yes."

I drop my hand and she curls her warm, soft palm around me. She rubs up and down, clearly having closely watched the way

I'd been masturbating, and I close my hand over hers as she places her other palm on my balls.

We both rub, my gaze on hers as she stares at my swollen cock. She wets her lips and that's it, I lose all control.

"Anna," I groan, as I shift, and shoot my load all over her lush breasts. She gasps as my liquid heat coats her and drips down her tits. I continue to squeeze, her palm still beneath mine as I milk every last drop. Once I'm depleted, I let go of her hand, and she puts her finger in my cum and swirls it around her tits. I nearly come again.

I fall over her, and find her mouth. She tastes so goddamn good, a guy could lose himself in her kisses. Christ, here I was worried sick about ruining her, when I really should have been worried about her ruining me.

I wake to the sound of Chase laughing outside, and I jolt up in my bed and check the clock. Oh no! I didn't set the alarm and slept in. I can't imagine my new boss—the same man that put his hands and mouth all over me last night and gave me incredible pleasure—will be too pleased with me. It's the weekend, but I'm still responsible for Chase. I think?

Jumping from my bed, I note that I'm naked, and my thoughts go back to last night. I snuggled into Alek after he came over my breasts and we stayed like that for a long time, until he finally broke the quiet, and cleaned me up as I was falling asleep. Afterward, he picked me up and carried me to my room, tucking me in before he retired to his own room.

My body tingles in memory as I dress quickly and tie my hair back. I hurry downstairs praying he doesn't fire me, and I dart outside into the warm sunshine. Alek is in the pool with Chase, and his eyes lock on mine as soon as he sees me.

"I'm sorry," I blurt out, so aware of his presence, and his near nakedness. God, I'm a frazzled mess.

He stares at me for so long, I begin to wonder if I have something on my face, or forgot a piece of clothing.

"How did you sleep?" he finally asks.

"So good I overslept. I'm sorry," I say again. I jerk my thumb over my shoulder. "I'll get started on breakfast."

"I can't stay. I have a meeting."

"It's Saturday."

"It's not a work meeting," he says to me, as he climbs from the pool, water dripping from his gorgeous body. Chase follows him out and I go to the cabinet and grab a couple of towels. I hand Alek his and I open Chase's and wrap it around him.

"Thanks, Anna." He smiles with a big toothy grin. "Can we have pancakes, please?"

I ruffle his wet hair. "Such a polite little boy, and of course we can have pancakes." I lift my head to find Alek watching me. "You're doing such a great job with him." I really want to ask about his mother, but I don't.

"Thanks."

Alek towel dries himself, and I try not to stare, try not to remember the feel of his hard muscles beneath my fingers. "You don't want to eat before you go?" I ask.

"I'll grab something out."

He heads inside and I follow him. Why is he acting so distant this morning? Does he think last night was a mistake? It was, of course. It goes completely against policy, but he can't deny that it was fun. Maybe it was just a one-time thing. Although he did say he was going to fuck me. But maybe he's having second thoughts this morning. I should be having second thoughts too.

Getting involved with him isn't smart. Cripes, I have no idea how far my parents would go to get me to do what they wish. They could use Alek and his son against me. That thought hits like a slap, and blood drains to my toes.

"Anna, are you okay?" I sink into a kitchen chair, and Alek curses under his breath. "You've gone white, and you look like you're going to pass out. You need to eat something." He pulls his phone from his pocket and my mind races—I've made a huge mistake—as he shoots off a text.

"No, I'm okay. I'm not feeling faint. I just thought of..." I let my words fall off. He doesn't need to know what was going through my mind, and if anyone touched a hair on his head or Chase's to get to me, I'd never forgive myself.

"Thought of what?"

I shake my head. "Nothing, it's nothing important."

He stares at me. He doesn't like liars, so if I don't open my mouth, I'm not lying, right?

Chase pushes on his stool and the scraping sound cuts through the silence as he slides it across the floor and goes to the sink to pour a glass of water. It spills over the edge as he climbs from his stool and comes my way. "Have some water, Anna."

I smile at his sweetness, my heart squeezing tight in my chest. God, I could fall for this little boy. "Thanks, bud," I say. I take a huge drink and I'm about to stand when Alek's strong hand lands on my shoulder to hold me down, and ohmigod, I shouldn't like that so much.

I blink up at him. "What are you doing?"

"I postponed my meeting until later. I'm cooking breakfast for you and Chase."

I give a fast shake of my head. "No. That's my job."

He holds me down, and even though Chase just ran into the other room, he lowers his voice. "Last night...I kept you up too late."

At the mention of last night, his eyes blaze hot, and my entire body reacts with want. "I didn't...mind. I liked it...sir."

The muscles along his jaw ripple as he clenches down. He curses under his breath, and I rein myself in as Chase comes running back into the room.

"Daddy, can we go see Gus today?"

"I don't know, maybe," Aleks says and stands. He checks his phone. "I'm not sure how long my meeting will take. Maybe Anna can take you?"

I frown. "Who's Gus?"

Chase laughs. "He's a turtle. He's hundreds of years old."

I grin. "That's old."

"He's a hundred years old," Alek explains. "He lives at the museum." He cocks his head. "Have you never been to the museum?"

I freeze. Crap. I hate to be out of the house too much. What if someone spots me? As a nanny, however, I have to take Chase places, and it would seem awfully suspicious if we never left the house. I quickly smile, not wanting Alek to worry about me, but secretly liking that he does.

"Of course, yes. I just didn't realize he was talking about the famous turtle. I think we could definitely go see Gus today."

Chase's big smile is like a warm blanket to my heart. Alek eyes me for a second, then goes to the cupboard and pulls out a frying pan. He places it on his state-of-the-art gas stove, and I salivate, loving that appliance so much.

"Do you like to cook?" I ask him.

"Not really. Do you?"

"Yes," I blurt out. "It's my dream to be a chef."

He turns back to me, his brow narrowed. "Really?"

Shoot, why did I tell him that? "Yeah," I say and give a wave of my hand like it's not all that important. "Someday I'll go to culinary school, but that's down the road."

"Have you applied anywhere?"

"Not yet. I'm saving up."

He pours batter from a box into a bowl and I try not to cringe. "What?" he asks. Obviously hiding my distain is hard.

I crinkle my nose in apology. "I make them from scratch."

"When you're feeling better, you can make them from scratch. When I'm making them, they come from a box."

"Fair enough."

He paused. "Coffee?"

"Yes, please, with just a splash of milk. I can get it."

He points the spatula at me. "Sit," he demands, and my damn nipples harden.

"Bossy much?"

He grins at me, and holy God, it's so hot and sensual, I'm about ready to climax again. "You just keep remembering I'm the boss and we'll get along just fine."

He pours me a cup, adds milk and hands it to me. "Do you cook for all your nannies?" I ask.

"No."

I don't know why I asked that, and I don't know why his answer makes me so happy. Okay, maybe I do know why. Maybe what I was really asking is if he treated his past nannies with such kindness and if he slept with them.

"Where do you want to go to culinary school?"

"The Culinary Institute of America. It's in New York." I take a sip of coffee as he adds water and an egg to the batter and whisks it.

"You don't want to go to school here in Chicago? I'm pretty sure we have some great culinary schools."

"We do. Kendall College is the best, but I want to explore other places, you know. I haven't really traveled a lot."

He pours the batter into a hot frying pan, and turns to me. "Are you from around here?"

"Yes." I look into my coffee cup, stare at it like it might hold the answers to world hunger.

"Your family is here?"

"Um, yeah. It's complicated. We don't...we just don't see eye to eye on everything. My father is old school. He thinks I should get married—he's trying to marry me off to some friend of the family's son, actually—but I want to be more than just some guy's wife." *Stop rambling Anna.* I try to shut my mouth, but then suddenly I'm spewing, "I want to live, see the world, go to Paris, experience...everything, you know?"

God what is wrong with me?

His eyes hold mine captive, and I know he's thinking about last night, and how he promised to show me everything. "I know."

Chase picks up a toy car and starts rolling it across the floor and into the other room. It breaks the tension between us. Alek goes back to the pancakes, and I note the jar on the counter again.

"What's the jar for?"

"It's a to-do jar. Things to do."

"You have an awful lot of things to do." I make a move to get up, but catch the way he's looking at me. "Can I see?"

"Of course you can see. It's for you." He picks the jar up and hands it to me. I pull the top off and pull out a slip of paper.

"This says go to the park." I smile in delight. "I thought it was going to be like a chore list."

"Keep going." He gestures with a nod for me to pick something else out.

I frown as I read it. "Dust under the beds."

"It can't be all fun and games."

I nod. "True. Am I allowed to add to the jar, or is that a boss thing?"

He makes a face that suggests he's never been asked that question before, and that my question might just be ludicrous. "No."

"Okey-doke." I guess he's pretty serious about keeping control over his jar, and I'd better not mess with it, other than to pull a chore. I shove it away. "How many do I pick a day?"

"Just one."

He plates a pancake. If I picked one and hated it, could I exchange it for something more pleasant? I consider it, but something tells me if our days were filled with fun, and no chores, he'd see through that in a minute.

"Chase, come get your breakfast," he calls out.

Chase comes running back into the room, and sits across from me. He pours a generous amount of syrup onto his pancake as Alek slides a plate in front of me. "Looks great," I say, injecting a measure of enthusiasm into my voice.

"Don't lie."

I chuckle. "Wait until you taste mine." I rub my stomach and moan, the sound not unlike the one I made last night when he touched me. "So delicious."

His eyes darken, his breathing a little more labored. "I'm sure anything of yours I put in my mouth would be delicious." As soon as the words fall off his tongue and he realizes how sexual they sounded, a groan crawls out of his throat.

"Are you okay, Daddy?" Chase asks.

"Yeah, just have something stuck in my throat," he says, and his phone pings. He picks it up and frowns as he reads the message.

"Everything okay?" I ask as I bite into the horrible pancake that tastes like sawdust.

He turns the stove off and washes his hands. "I have to get dressed and go." He pulls a credit card from his wallet and sets it on the table. "This is for you, and anything you might need. Groceries, clothes, anything for Chase, and for God's sake, get yourself a bathing suit that fits."

I bite my lip, because I think he might have liked that floppy bathing suit and just isn't admitting it.

"The SUV is in the garage." He pauses and stares at me. "You do drive, right?"

"Yes, of course."

"The keys are in the bowl by the front door. Can I have your phone, please?"

My heart goes completely still, and blood drains to my feet. Why would he want my phone? The incessant ringing has slowed since I came here last night, but there must be a hundred unanswered texts and phone calls from my father. I don't want him to see any of those.

"I...I'm not even sure where I left it." He hates liars. I'm lying, and he damn well knows it. I make light of it. "Last night, I think I set it down somewhere."

He holds my gaze a second longer, and it's true. Last night was a whirlwind of awesome sex and I could have set it anywhere.

"Fine." He pulls his from his pocket. "Put your contact information in here." I do as he asks and he shoots me off a text. "When you find your phone, please respond."

"You didn't eat. Here at least have a bite." I cut off a big slice of pancake and hold it out to him.

He glares at me, his look stern and hard, and while he's authoritative like the men I've grown up around, there's more to him. Something sweet, and soft—although I'd never tell him that. He passes that trait on to his son, and believe me, it's a good thing.

"You're the one who needs to eat."

"You need to eat too, Alek."

His gaze holds mine, and for a second I think he's going to refuse, but then his mouth opens and I slide the fork in. He moans his approval, his eyes meeting mine. Everything in his gaze tells me he's hungry, but not for pancakes. Honest to God, this man is going to eat me alive and if I knew what was good for me, I'd bail now. I can't—won't—put him and his son in danger, which means I need to make good decisions, and put a stop to this thing between us.

I just have to figure out how...

8

ALEK

I head outside, my stomach in knots. Jesus, a guy should be able to meet his parents without feeling like he's going to vomit. Of course, they wanted to see Chase today, they always do, and I want them to be a part of his life, but I thought he'd have a better day with Anna. While my parents don't say much in front of him, he always picks up on my tension, and I'd like to shelter him from that today when I'm breaking in a new nanny. I mean...ugh. Okay, maybe that didn't come out right. Nevertheless, I save Chase's visits for family gatherings, or necessary babysitting, not one-on-one interrogations. That's exactly what's going to happen today.

I drive to my parents' home and go through the impenetrable gate. I'm met with guards, who usher me inside my childhood home. I instantly feel claustrophobic as I'm led through the house to the backyard, where my father is sitting around a table with a group of men. As soon as he sees me, he dismisses them all and tells them to let my mother, Alisa, know I'm here.

"Dad," I say, and smooth my hand down my tie as I sit.

"Alek, it's so nice to see you. Have you eaten?"

"I'm not hungry."

"At least have some coffee." He snaps his fingers and a servant rushes to me with a mug and a carafe full of coffee. I give a nod and she pours. "How are you, son? Where's Chase?"

"He's getting to know his new nanny."

Dad frowns. "Again. What happened to the last one?"

"I have no idea. Do you?"

"Why would I know what happened to your nanny?"

Oh, because he keeps a closer eye on my life than he lets on. Sometimes I think my ex disappeared because of him, but I have no proof, and only received the divorce papers in the mail.

"Alek." Mom smiles, coming out onto the deck in a coral, summery dress that flares around her knees. "Son, look at you." She takes my face in her hands and kisses my cheeks. "Where's Chase?"

"He's with his new nanny," my father answers before I can.

Mom's dark eyes widen. "Oh, he has a new nanny. Maxim, did you know about this?"

"Of course not," he says, and their surprised reaction eases the tension inside me. They're both either very good actors, or they really know nothing about my last nanny's sudden exit. I'm leaning toward the latter. Why would they want to get rid of someone Chase adored? It wouldn't make sense.

My father opens his mouth, and I cut him off. "She comes from the agency. You don't need to do a background check on her."

"We can never be too—"

"I've got this handled."

He goes quiet, and I prepare for a protest. But he relaxes, stands and pulls a chair out for Mom. My father might be a lot of things, but he treats Mom like a princess. She smiles at Dad, and he pours her a cup of coffee. Her spoon clinks as she adds sugar, and I shift restlessly, waiting for the inquisition.

"Chase starts school soon," Mom says.

I nod. "He's excited."

"Do you think he has enough of a female presence in his life?"

Here we go.

"He has you, doesn't he?"

"It's not like you bring him by a lot, Alek."

"He has a new nanny. She's really good with him and he likes her."

"I do think it's time he had more stability." She gives a disappointed shake of her head. "The way you go through nannies…"

I take a sip of coffee and it rises back in my throat. "I just want what's best for him, Mom."

"Which is why you need to get married. There's this girl—"

"Mom," I warn.

Her brow lifts, a challenge in her eyes. "I believe your exact words were, I'm not a great judge of character when it comes to women."

Why did I open my big mouth and say that?

"I was going through a hard time."

"Son," Mom begins and puts her hand over mine. "We only want what's best for you and Chase. I know you well, I know the kind of woman you *should* marry." She puts emphasis on the word should, a reminder that I'd messed up in the past. "If you'd just hear me out, I know you'd like her."

"I'm not a child who needs his mother to pick his clothes anymore, Mom."

"A wife is far more important than clothes, Alek, and you must admit I did a fine job with your wardrobe. I think you should trust me when it comes to matters of the heart. I know a good match when I see one. Isn't that right, darling?" She looks at Dad, and they smile at each other. While I love that they have a good relationship—and it was an arranged one—it doesn't mean a set-up will work for me.

"Mom—"

She blinks thick lashes coated in mascara at me. "Well, this girl is sweet. I was talking to her mother just the other day. We both think you'd be a great pair, her name is—"

"I don't care what her name is. I'm not interested."

"Let me show you a picture of her."

"No."

Dad releases an impatient sigh. No one messes with my father, but I'm his son, and that gives me a special place in his heart. Still, I can only get away with so much, and for so long. Deep in my gut, I know I'm going to cave, and one day walk down the aisle with a woman of their choice. Honestly, they've been so good to me. A son is supposed to follow in his father's footsteps, but they didn't force that on me. They protected me and let me live my own life. I'm not sure why, and I'm not asking questions, and I just want to have a nice cup of coffee with the people I love.

"How about I think about it?" I appease my Mom and a big smile curls up her lips.

"Perfect." She leans in and kisses me on the cheek again. "Now tell me everything that has been going on."

We spend the next hour talking, and then Dad and I head to the small golf course at the back of his property and play all nine holes. Once we're done, I pull my phone from my pocket to check for any messages from Anna. All I see is a message from earlier, telling me she got my message, so she now has me in her contacts. At least she found her phone. Truthfully, I thought she was going to bite off her tongue when I asked for it. Once again, an uneasy feeling closes in on me. Who is Anna, and who is she running from? I glance at my dad as he puts his club into the bag. For a second, I consider asking him to do a more thorough search, but decide against it. I'm a grown-ass man. I can take care of things myself, and the less meddling on his part, the better. I can't see it leading to anything good.

I wipe a bead of sweat from my forehead. "I'm going to take off."

"So soon?" my father asks, as he checks his phone, just as distracted as I am. He wants to get back to work, and I'm hoping to meet up with Anna and Chase at the museum.

"Yeah, I have some things to take care of."

"You'll think about what we talked about?"

Marrying a stranger. Yeah. Sure. Right after I hang myself.

"I told you I would." I glance up at the house, giving the only answer I can give to temporarily keep the peace. "I'll go say goodbye to Mom." I put my club into the bag, and pull on my suit jacket. I shoot Anna off a text, hoping I'm not too late to join them. I'll have to stop at home and change first.

After giving Mom a kiss goodbye and promising to bring Chase by soon, I head home. An odd sensation tingles along my spine as I pull into my driveway and kill my ignition. The house looks like it's locked up, but it always does. I pop the garage and the SUV is gone. I check my phone again, but still no message from Anna. Why isn't she answering?

I kill the ignition and climb from the car. Back in the house, I dress in casual khaki shorts and a colored polo, but as I move through the house, I once again have a strange sensation. I glance over my shoulder, expecting someone to be there, but the place is empty.

Okay, I'm getting paranoid. Sometimes my visits to my father's with all his security can do that to me. Then again, I'd have to be a fool to think he didn't have a tail on me at all times. I'm the son of a powerful man, someone who could be used against him, and I'm sure I'm always under a watchful eye, which means they would have known about Anna. Maybe that's the noise Anna heard in the yard that night. Maybe it wasn't me at all, but one of Dad's men doing a check on someone with access to me. I guess she must have come up clean otherwise Dad would have run her out of town.

Walking to my window I glance out, my gaze going to the neighbors, and I try not to visualize the first time I caught a glimpse of Anna half naked. She is so goddamn gorgeous, it's no wonder I couldn't keep my hands off her. I should have been stronger, though. I'm her goddam boss, and this is an insane game we're playing but I like it. A lot. I'm about to push away from the window when I spot Theresa. She's on the phone and looking through the fence into my backyard.

Cracking my window, even though whoever she's talking to and whatever she's saying is none of my business, I lean out slightly. Her words are low, whispered, clearly not meant for my ears, but she keeps glancing over her shoulder, and that body language is strange to me. Not my business, though. At least I don't think it is.

My phone rings, and I pull it from my pocket. I slide my finger across the screen.

"Anna."

"Hi Alek."

She sounds winded, breathless, like she'd been running. Alarm bells jangle. She's been so spooked I can't help but wonder if she's not running away from someone. "Is everything okay?" I ask working to sound calm. "Is Chase okay?"

"Perfectly fine. We did a bit of shopping, and Chase and I went to the park. We kicked a ball around, and I think he wore me out."

I chuckle. "I told you, you needed your energy."

Her soft laugh curls around me and strokes my dick. "You were right about that."

"You haven't gone to see Gus yet?" I try to keep the hope from my voice. No need for her to know how much I want to see her.

"No, we were about to get ice cream and head over. We can... wait for you."

"Yeah?"

"Of course. Instead of ice cream, maybe we can find one of those old fashioned ice cream trucks like when you were a kid and get the rocket popsicles. I know how much you love them, and I bet you could use one today. It's a scorcher."

Jesus, is she for real? My heart does some ridiculous thump against my chest. I have no idea why, but I really like the thoughts of her waiting for me. It's not just that, it's the longing in her voice, like she wants to see me, but that could just be my imagination. Maybe the sex—or lack thereof—is messing with me, and maybe it's because I haven't had a woman other than my mother show any kind of kindness to me in a long time.

"Old fashioned ice cream truck?" I laugh. "How old do you think I am, anyway?"

Her adorable chuckle comes through the phone teasing my aching dick. "Just teasing, Alek. It's not like you're old enough to be my daddy."

Fuck me, twice.

"Can you hurry, though? I'm not sure how long I can hold Chase off."

I check the time. "I can be there in fifteen minutes." Ten if I don't take five minutes to tug one out.

"Hey, Alek." Her voice is low, and throaty again, and I'm about to tell her to make it twenty, because it's possible I might need to tug two out.

"Yeah."

"Maybe we can find one that's red, white and green."

A grin spreads across my face, no doubt reaching both ears. God, I like her.

"Smart ass."

"See you soon."

I end the call and run through the house like a starving boy called to the dinner table. A short while later, I park my car, and walk into the park. Numerous people are out running the trails with their pets, playing ball with their kids, or eating snacks on a blanket. A strange sense of longing rockets through me. Is Chase missing out on having a real family because I'm so damn jaded?

A mother picks her son up, and spins him around. They both laugh loudly, and he throws his arms around her as she kisses him on the head. The sight tugs at my heart, and my pulse beats a little faster in my throat. Maybe I really should give Mom's suggestion deeper consideration.

Food trucks line the streets, all the vendors vying for the dollar. I scan for an ice cream truck, but my search comes up empty. Grabbing my phone, I'm about to shoot off a text to Anna to find out exactly where they are, when I hear Chase.

"Daddy, Daddy."

I lift my head to find him running toward me. Anna is glancing around, keeping a slight distance. I follow her gaze, and find nothing but families having fun. My attention strays back to her, and I take in the soft sway of her hips. She'd changed into a loose-fitting dress that sends my imagination into overdrive.

"Everything okay?" I ask as she turns back to me.

She smiles. "Perfectly fine."

"Were you looking for someone?"

She shakes her head. "Just enjoying the day. How was your meeting?"

"Good. Dad and I played a round of golf." Shit, I hadn't meant to bring up my father.

"You call seeing your family a meeting?" she asks.

"There was some business we needed to discuss." She nods in understanding, and Chase tugs on my shirt.

"You saw Grandma and Grandpa?"

"Yes, and you'll see them soon too, Chase." I don't miss the way Anna is watching us, taking in the exchange. I change the subject. "Who's up for ice cream?"

"Me," Chase screams.

"Me too." I take Chase's hand and Anna moves in beside us, close, but not close enough to think we're all together.

"Anna," Chase says and holds his hand out. "Swing me."

She hesitates for a brief second, does a fast glance around and comes a bit closer. Chase squeals as we swing him, and a smile lights up Anna's face. Does she want a family of her own someday? I know she said her family life was complicated—hell, mine is too—but she's so good with Chase. Good with me, too. But I don't take her as the fairy tale kind of girl who used to watch Disney as she plotted her own big theatrical wedding.

"Did you go shopping?" I ask.

"We did. We got a few pool toys Chase wanted."

Toys.

My mind goes off in another direction at the mention of toys. My sweet, and innocent girl has never used toys. Maybe it's time to change that.

"Did you get yourself a couple of bathing suits?"

"No," she says, a blush on her cheeks. "I didn't want to leave Chase alone while I was in the change room trying on swim suits."

I nod, and my dick thickens thinking about her in lingerie. "Right, I never thought of that." I snort. "It's a good thing I have you doing the thinking for me."

A good thing indeed, because when I'm around her, it's all I can do to keep my blood from draining south. Maybe once I fuck her, that problem will rectify itself.

Or maybe it will just make it worse.

9

ANNA

Chase talks a mile a minute as we head home after a fun time at the museum. I have no idea how he can still keep his eyes open. I'm freaking exhausted, and in desperate need of a nap. I pull into the driveway, and press the button on the rearview mirror to pop the garage. I drive the vehicle into the huge garage, like I've done it a million times before. It makes me feel like this is actually my home, a place where I belong and it pushes back the loneliness inside me and makes me think there might be a place for me in this world. But I'd be wise to remember that I don't belong anywhere. I never have.

Hopefully one day, after I've had a few more life experiences, that sense of loss and hurt will be nothing but a distant memory. I also hope someday my parents and I can reconcile and they'll come to realize pushing me into marriage for their personal gain is wrong. Sadly, I'm not sure I'll ever see that happening, no matter how much I want it, or how much I miss them.

I click the button on the rearview mirror to close the garage as Alek pulls into the driveway. Since the booster seat was in the SUV, it only made sense that Chase come home with me, and I kind of like that Alek trusts me with him. My heart does a little jump when I catch Alek's smile in the mirror before the door fully shuts.

Remember, Anna. You have to stay strong and keep your distance. Physically and emotionally.

At that reminder, I exit the vehicle, about to get Chase out, but he unbuckles and jumps from the back seat, all the while talking about how much he wants a turtle. My God, little boys are much busier than little girls. Alek's voice comes from inside the house, and I stifle a yawn as I enter.

"Hey," he says. "Tired?"

"I'm fine," I fib, but I don't think too much gets by him.

"Why don't you go have a rest." He puts his hands on my shoulder like he's about to turn me. The touch is innocent, and shouldn't arouse me, but it does, and there isn't much I can do about it. "I'll order in for dinner."

"Actually, I want to cook. I've been dying to use your gorgeous stove."

His knuckles brush mine and sends heat zapping through me. "You sure?"

I try not to sound breathless, when I answer. "Positive."

"Okay, but how about if I help?"

"You don't have to do that."

He just grins at me and we walk down the hall. Chase is plunked on the sofa playing video games. "Hungry, little man?" Alek asks.

"I want a turtle, Daddy."

"For dinner?" Alek teases and I grin, loving the relationship he has with his son.

Chase rolls on the sofa and laughs. "No, that's gross. I want a pet turtle."

"How about we discuss that later?"

"Can I have chicken nuggets?"

Alek laughs. "He always wants chicken nuggets. They're not the healthiest of foods, and I do try to do healthy."

"I know, you were going for the apples when I met you, remember?"

"I remember."

"Chase is getting his chicken nuggets, and he won't even know they're healthy. In fact, he'll love them better than take out."

"Yeah?"

"You sound skeptical," I say, a challenge in my voice. I'm so sure of myself, I add, "You want to make a wager?"

"You called me old today, Anna." He shoves his hands into his pockets and leans toward me. "Now you're asking if I want to make a *wager*, like I'm some wild west cowboy."

"I do love an old western."

"Really?"

I laugh. "Yes, I used to watch them with—" I stop talking. Abruptly. He stands there staring at me, and I mentally shake my head. My God this man has the ability to throw me off balance without even trying. I was seconds from telling him I used to watch them with Dad's guard Antonio. "I used to watch them all the time."

"That surprises me."

"I'm full of surprises."

I'm full of something.

"Wait, why does that surprise you?" I ask. "Did you think I was the Disney princess kind of girl?"

He dips his head, all teasing gone from his eyes. My heart lurches at the sudden intensity about him. Thank God this guy is a friend because while there is a genuine kindness to him, there is a fierceness there too—a warning: do not mess with me. It's exciting, and exhilarating, and I shouldn't like it as much as I do. I know better than that. Especially since I've been around powerful men my whole life, men who take what they want, without asking, and don't care who they destroy in the process.

"No, and that's too bad. I want that for you."

Ohmigod. That is not at all the answer I expected. His dark eyes narrow in on me, looking too carefully, too closely. I can't, won't let him see the real me, so I plaster on a smile and say, "Good. Now about this wager..."

He grins, and the mood once again lightens.

"What do you have in mind?"

Shit, what am I doing? Didn't I already give myself a hard lecture about backing away from him? Why can't I seem to do it? What is it about him that makes me needy, maybe even a bit reckless?

Like running away wasn't reckless enough, Anna.

I had no choice about that, but getting involved with Alek... well, I do have a choice there. I think.

"Can I think on it?" I ask and I'm about to turn, to take the chicken I've been thawing from the fridge—yes, Chase asked earlier today if we could have nuggets for dinner. He curls his fingers around my wrist and stops me, and I take in a breath.

"No."

"No," I repeat quietly. "I can't think on it?"

His grin is slow, almost dangerous, and my entire body reacts with want. "You're the one who asked for the wager, which means I get to set the terms."

"Oh." Oh, God. "What did you have in mind?"

"If he hates the nuggets, later tonight I get to do whatever I want to you."

"Are you...going to fuck me?" A hard quake goes through me, my nipples tightening as I recall the way he said he would take me so hard I'd still feel him a week later.

You don't want that, girl.

Oh, but I do, I really do.

Instead of answering, he continues with, "If he loves them, the night plays out the way you want it."

"Do you have the western station?" I ask, and he grins at me.

"No, but I can probably order something up for you. Speaking of ordering..." His voice falls off and his brow furrows. "I'll be right back, okay? I have a few things to take care of."

Wow, talk about a one-eighty. He went from playful to serious in seconds. He walks off and I instantly miss his presence. I give myself a hard lecture to keep myself together, and get to work on making the best nuggets Chase has ever had. As I soak them in buttermilk, the sudden urge to destroy them, to make them taste awful tugs at me and I can't believe I would purposely sabotage them so Alek would win the wager.

If, I mean *when* I win, how will I want the night to play out?

Footsteps sound behind me, and my entire body reacts to Alek's presence. "What can I do?" he asks, his voice close to my ear, his warm breath on my neck.

"I noticed you have an air fryer. Do you want to make some fries?"

"The air fryer and I aren't friends, Anna. There was an incident."

"What?" I laugh and turn to him. He has a sheepish grin on his face. "What did you do?"

"I tried to do fries once, and half were burnt, half was undercooked, and the other half were just tasteless."

"You don't have three halves, Alek," I say laughing. "Sounds like you crowded it. Here, let me show you." I wipe my hands on a towel, and as the chicken soaks in buttermilk, I spend the next fifteen minutes showing Alek how to make the perfect French fry.

"How did you get so good in the kitchen, again?" he asks.

"It's a passion." I pause for a second. "We all have a passion, right?" I take the chicken, and add it to the batter, coat it and place it on a tray. "What's your passion, Alek?"

He goes quiet. "Between work and Chase, I don't have much time to myself."

"That's understandable." I set the oven and place the nuggets inside. "Before Chase, what did you like to do?"

"In the winter, I love snowboarding and skiing."

"That sounds like fun."

"You've never done it?"

"No." I don't bother to tell him I grew up sheltered with very few friends.

"Were you raised by nuns or something?"

I give a humorless laugh. "Something like that. I guess that's why I'd like to experience those activities."

"There are a lot of things you need to experience."

He has his back to me as he takes a bottle of wine from the rack and opens it, so I can't tell if he's bringing the subject back around to sex. He pours us each a glass and I arch a brow when he hands me one.

"I'm not legal drinking age."

"Shit, right."

I take the glass from him, and laugh. "I can get married, but I can't have a sip of wine. How's that for logic?"

"You really hate the idea of marriage, huh?"

I lean against the counter. "Yes and no. I just...have so much to do you know. Maybe my priorities would change if the right guy came along."

"Your priorities don't have to change. They shouldn't. The right guy would want you to do all the things you want to do."

"You think?"

"Sure, he'd want you to go to school, get a culinary degree, open your own business when you're ready. Travel. See Paris. You shouldn't miss out on anything."

I smile and nod, enjoying this easy conversation with him. I like getting to know Alek on a personal level, even though that's not the job of a nanny. Yeah, like sleeping with him fits the job description. I guess we already crossed a lot of lines. "Do you feel like you've missed out on anything?"

"I love my son, and wouldn't change a thing where he's concerned."

"I know you love him. It's easy to see that." He smiles at me and my heart squeezes.

"I just feel like he's missing out. On having a mom. I want to do right by him, which is why..."

I move a bit closer. "Why what?"

"Why my parents are insisting I get married." He snorts. "They think they have the perfect wife for me."

I take a sip of wine, and hate the jealous sensations rising up in me. "God, what is it with meddling parents, anyway?"

"No idea. I guess things were done differently in their generation."

"Not my business, but I'm guessing that's what you had to discuss with them today."

"Yup, I told them I'd think about it. I'm probably going to need an MRI."

"What?" I ask. What is he talking about?

"I must have a tumor or something."

I laugh, and not wanting to think about depressing things, I switch topics. "What fun things do you do in the summer?"

"I have a cottage. Lake Geneva."

My eyes go wide. "Why would you ever leave this house? It has everything."

He laughs. "It doesn't have a lake, or water skiing, or fishing, and it's not totally secluded. I can see into my neighbor's pool and vice versa."

A wave of want goes through me at the reminder. "We should go," I blurt out without thinking.

Talk about overstepping, Anna.

"Yeah? That's something you'd like to do?"

"I mean, if you love your cottage, maybe you and Chase should go. It could be a really nice thing to do before he starts school." I glance at the to-do jar. "I have that thing to work through."

"I actually have a jar there. Although, I have yet to bring any of Chase's nannies. It's mostly for repairs I need to do. Things like that. It keeps me on track."

"Would you be able to get the time off work?"

"I could bring work with me, and honestly, I could use a break, especially after agreeing to think over marriage. I don't know what I was thinking."

"You were thinking you wanted to get your parents off your back."

"You're right." He pauses. "It's a bad idea, isn't it?"

"Letting your parents pick out your spouse? Yeah, Alek, that's a very bad idea, and why I'm..." He arches a brow. "Ah, well, that's the reason I'm not really talking to mine right now. But you should go, get away. It will do you good."

"You should come." He moves an inch closer, and his warm scent washes over me. I breathe him in and note the chain reaction in my body.

Truthfully, going to the lake might be a good idea, considering I'm hiding out and it sounds like he has a secluded place. But on the other hand, I can probably find a way to keep a measure of distance between us in this big house. At the lake, I might not be so lucky.

"I don't want to impose."

"Chase will need his nanny," he murmurs, not even bothering to hide the desire in his eyes, or voice.

I swallow. God, I'm supposed to be keeping my distance, right? "It could be good father-son time."

"Okay, then. *I* might need my son's nanny."

Way to put it right out there, although he didn't need words. His body, the heat in his eyes speaks volumes. He puts his hand on my side, splays his fingers. His thumb lightly brushes the side of my breast, and I nearly lose all ability to stand.

"Might?" *God, what are you doing, girl?*

"I do," he murmurs. "I need my son's nanny."

"Alek..."

"I'm the boss, remember. You do as I say."

"I remember, sir."

He curses under his breath as I bite back a smile. God, I love how I can reduce this big, strong intimidating man to a hot mess of need. It's empowering. I have never in my life had such confidence in myself or inner strength. I like it a lot. I like how he's not afraid of me drawing on that strength. Strength in women can intimidate the men in my world, but it doesn't intimidate him. Just then, the timer on the oven goes off and Chase comes running into the room.

"I'm hungry."

Alek backs off and I bite my lip as he adjusts his shorts. "You have great timing, kiddo."

"That's right," I agree as we share a secret chuckle, one that says Chase's timing is the worst. "Dinner is ready. I made you chicken nuggets."

Chase puts his hands around my waist and hugs me, not at all afraid of showing his emotions. God, this feels so nice, so real. My heart goes still in my chest, and I silently warn myself to be careful and not to get too invested in this family.

"You're the best, Anna," Chase says.

I lift my head to find Alek watching us and I take a breath to get my heart beating again. Okay, pull it together. Get the meal on the table. You're the nanny, nothing else, and that's what nannies do.

A few minutes later we're all seated at the table, and Chase grabs a nugget from the big pile and takes a huge bite. He chews for a moment, and looks the nugget over, like he's assessing it—trying to decide if it is indeed a nugget. It's definitely not what he's used to.

Alek and I exchange a glance, both waiting on the verdict.

"What do you think, little man?" Alek asks and takes a bite out of his own. His eyes go wide. "Anna, these are delicious. How did you make them so tender and crispy without frying them?"

"That's a secret," I tease.

"Anna, these are the best nuggets I've ever had," Chase says, and a wide smile splits my lips.

Alek shakes his head, a grin on his handsome face. "I guess it's western night at the Hail house."

Hail.

Apparently, he does have a last name. He, of course, found mine out when he had to call the agency to let them know he hired me. Although it's not my real last name. I can't ask him who he really is when I'm hiding who I really am.

"You should definitely open your own restaurant."

I give him a cocky grin. "If you think my nuggets are good, wait until you taste my shrimp scampi."

"I can't wait to taste everything," Alek says, and I try not to take it sexually. My body on the other hand... it's warming in all the wrong—or right—places as it thinks about Alek taking a taste. Needing to cut the sexual tension before we blow up the kitchen, I turn to Chase. We talk about our trip to the museum, as we continue to eat and once we're done, I stand to take care of the dishes.

"I need to get Chase ready for bed."

"I can do that right after dishes," I tell him.

"No, I like doing it." The doorbell rings, and I nearly jump out of my skin.

"Whoa are you okay?"

I play it off. "Yeah, just startled me."

He stares at me for a few minutes and there are so many questions in his eyes. He doesn't ask, and I'm grateful. Instead, he says, "I'll get the door, and get Chase off to bed."

The two head down the hall, and I tip toe to the archway and hold my breath as he opens the door. Relief moves through me when I spot a delivery driver. I hurry back to the sink, not wanting Alek to know I was spying on him.

I finish the dishes as Alek finishes up with Chase, and I flop down onto the sofa, flicking through the stations when he comes back.

"Find any good westerns?" he asks, and sits beside me, a grin on his face.

"Not yet."

I flick through the stations, and he eventually puts his hand over mine to take the remote. His hand is firm and warm on mine, and an audible gasp falls from my lips.

"You're going so fast you're making me dizzy."

"You do like slow, don't you?" Ohmigod, did I really just say that?

"When it comes to some things, yes."

I stare at him, take in the darkening of his eyes, and my nipples pucker, wanting his hot wet mouth on them again. One big palm lands on my cheek and I lean into it, already addicted to his touch and craving it more than I thought possible. He leans toward me, brushes his lips over mine.

"Anna, I want you."

While I love his openness and honesty, my lids fall shut and I can't help but ask. "Are you sure about this?"

"Not even a little."

My eyes open, and I catch him gazing at my mouth, a new kind of hunger about him. "Same."

"Do you want me to stop? I'll stop if you want me to. You know that, right?"

"I don't ever want anything bad..." I stop myself, unable to tell him anymore.

He stiffens, and it's insane how fast the want in his eyes shifted to something murderous. "Anna?"

"Nothing."

"If you're worried about something, I want to know."

"What if...the agency finds out." There's more to it, obviously. But I use the agency as an excuse. "I don't want anything bad to happen to you." That, right there, is the honest to God's truth.

He doesn't back away. Instead, he moves closer, offering me warmth and comfort and for the first time in a long time, I feel safe and secure. I think that's what I like most about him. This man can be fierce and dangerous but he's protective of those he cares about.

"Is that why you sort of stood back today, at the park?" he asks.

Jesus, it's hard to get anything by him. "You could get in trouble," I say. Not a lie, but not the whole reason either.

"Do you want me?" There's something in his eyes, a vulnerability that wraps around my heart and urges me to take him into my arms and make everything all right—for him. But I can't. It does, however, make me wonder what really happened between him and Chase's mother. Did she hurt him? Leave him broken and jaded? I'm not the girl who can put him back together again, and while sex is not smart, I do want him.

"I want you," I say, sensing he needs to hear those words, for reasons I'm not at all sure of. "We just need to be really careful. If anything happened to you, or Chase because of me..." I pause and shake my head. "I'd never forgive myself."

He stares at me, and I sense he wants to tell me something. "Anna, you have nothing to worry about, okay. My family..." He frowns, and the muscles in his jaw ripple as he clenches down. "Let's just say, nothing bad is going to happen to me or Chase, and you're safe with me. I promise, okay?"

I nod in agreement, even though I want to believe I'm safe, I know the power my family wields. As for his, I have no idea who they are, and truthfully, if he knew who mine was, he'd send me packing so fast it would make my head spin.

But right now, as he runs his fingers up and down my arm, I can't think about any of that. I want him. I can tell myself it's because it will ruin me for another, devalue me in the eyes of my family and in the eyes of their rivals. I have to tell myself that. Thinking there is more here is ludicrous, a fantasy. I'm a girl who lives in reality. My life, Alek's, and his son's life, depend on it. I really should say no, I'm not sure why, but I think that might mess with Alek in harmful ways, and he's been so sweet to me.

"I won the wager," I whisper.

"I know." His mouth is so close to mine, his breath comes hard and fast. "You changed your mind on the western?"

My body ignites as he lightly trails his fingers down my arm. "I have a confession, though."

"A confession?"

I shrug. "You asked me to be honest with you, so I have no choice but to admit there was no way you could win."

"Really."

"Yeah, you see, I perfected the chicken nugget ages ago. I set you up for failure."

"So, in a way, you cheated. That's what you're telling me?"

I nod, and exhale, like I'm sorry. "It's possible, and well, cheaters get eliminated."

His grin is wicked, hot and needy. "Which makes me the winner."

I do love a man who catches on quickly. "My thoughts exactly."

I stand, and her body is a quivering mess of want as I scoop her up. Mumbled curses rumble in my throat, warning me to slow the fuck down when all I want to do is rip the clothes off her and seat my dick high inside her. Fuck yeah.

Her hands go around my neck and her fast breaths warm my face as she struggles to get her breathing under control. I carry her up the stairs, bypass her room and take her straight to mine. Which is odd, because my room is my sanctuary, and not a single woman has set foot in it since my ex left.

Her eyes go wide as I quietly close the door and set the lock. I put her down, and back her up until she's pressed against the door. "What should I do with my sweet little virgin tonight?" I tease, and run my thumb over her bottom lip, tugging on it slightly.

"I think the terms of the wager were, you get to do anything you want," she replies and my cock jumps in my shorts. She wiggles her hot little body against my thickening appendage, and moans with need. "Please, Alek…"

"How can you beg for something you've never had before? How do you know you'll even like it?"

"Because you wouldn't have it any other way."

Her words catch me by surprise. She hasn't known me long, but she's right. When I give it to her, she's going to be ready and begging, and she's going to love it.

"You think you're ready for my cock?"

She gulps. "I do."

"Poor baby is hurting?"

I run my fingers from her neck, between her breasts down to her stomach, until I reach the hem of the dress that's been sending my imagination into overdrive. I slide my hand up her leg, and she makes whimpering sounds as I lightly stroke her.

"Have you been thinking about what my cock would feel like inside you?"

"God, yes."

"You want it in here?" I tug her panties to the side and slide a finger into her damp sex. Jesus, I never expected to find her this wet. I love it. I lightly fuck her with my finger, going deep and then staying still.

"Alek," she whimpers, and she grabs my shoulder as her legs give a little. "Please more…"

"I'm not so sure you're ready for more, Anna, and I'm not going to do anything before you're ready." I wiggle my finger inside her pussy, and her muscles clench around me. Fuck man, my size will destroy her. She's far too tight for me to go at her like a rutting animal, which is exactly what I want to do.

She whimpers, and lightly pounds my chest, but she has nothing to worry about. I plan to give her all kinds of pleasure tonight, just not with my throbbing cock. Maybe I'll let her suck me off this time, though. I have a feeling she's not going to let me get away without her pleasuring me somehow. She's definitely a give and take kind of girl.

"Alek...I need..."

To ease the ache inside her, I pull my finger from her cunt, slide it back in and say, "That doesn't mean I'm not going to get you ready, though."

"Yes." I kiss her again, a little harder, a fierce hunger clawing at me, urging me to simply give her what she wants and fuck her here and now, but I fight it off. I break the kiss and she's breathless, and I don't miss the question lingering in her lust-imbued eyes.

"What?" I ask, stilling my finger. "You know I like honesty, so if you have something to say, say it."

"Have you...been thinking about my...pussy?"

Sweet mother of God.

Okay, I guess I asked for that. "Yeah, baby. I've been thinking about this hot pussy since I first set eyes on you. It pretty much consumes me."

"What have you been thinking?" she asks, genuinely curious. The adventurous side combined with her innocent side is enough to do a man in.

I fuck her with my finger. Short blunt strokes that make her eyes go wide. "I've been thinking about all the ways I can touch you and bring you pleasure."

"I want that. I want..." Her eyes latch on me. "You."

Hearing her say that messes with my brain and prompts me into action. I pull my finger from her hot cunt, and her whimper of disappointment curls around me as I put my arms around her and carry her to my bed.

She sits and I stand there. Her mouth parts slightly and that's exactly where I want my cock.

"Have you ever sucked a cock before?"

I release the button on my shorts and excitement moves into her eyes. "No."

"But you want to?"

Her eyes lift. "I want to suck yours, Alek."

My legs nearly give out. I release my zipper, and push clothes down until my cock is free. She makes a whimpering little sound as I take my cock into my hands.

"I want to touch you." There's a bit of a command in her voice, and I like it. Sweet, little Anna is holding her own against me tonight. "I want to taste you."

I step up to her, take her hand and put it on my cock. I don't guide her. No, this time I let her explore and try not to shoot off in her face as she looks at my dick with pure adoration. Would she look at another guy's dick with such interest and fascination? I clench down on my teeth as that thought hits. What she does with anyone else is none of my business and I'm not about to make it my business.

"When you're here with me," I find myself stating. "No other guys, okay? Not even thoughts of them."

"Okay," she agrees readily. "Can I ask for the same?"

"I promise not to be with any other guy." She grins up at me and I go serious. ""I'm not with any other woman, Anna. I haven't been with any other woman for a long time."

Her smile is a mix of happiness, and wonderment. "Why me?" she asks, and I get it. I asked her the same question.

"I like you."

"Yeah, you said."

Honestly, I don't know what is driving me here. For the longest time, I wasn't interested in women, and if I needed relief, I'd tug one out. What is driving me to ruin this sweet girl, and maybe myself? I should be ashamed of myself, really. Taking something that doesn't really belong to me.

Ah, but she wants you, Alek, and you want to give her what she wants, and well, there's a part of you that needs to be wanted too.

Clearly that's the reason I'm not thinking straight.

"After you flashed me at the pool..." I reach down and lightly brush my thumbs over her breasts. "I knew I had to have a taste. You are so perfect."

"Hey," she blurts out, her hand tightening on my dick and it feel so good. "You said you didn't see anything when I *accidently* flashed you."

"Small lie."

"You said you didn't like liars."

"I was sparing your feelings, and Anna, can you take your dress off? I want to see all of you when I slide my cock into your mouth."

She gulps and her hand falls from my dick. I stroke myself as she makes quick work of her dress, leaving on her underwear."

"Bra must go."

She unhooks it, and a moan full of appreciation crawls out of my throat. "So perfect."

"These?" She takes her breasts into her hands and massages them.

"Yes," I growl. She briefly closes her eyes as she rubs her breasts, running the soft pads of her thumbs over her pretty pink nipples. My entire body vibrates, heat and need gripping my balls.

"Anna...please...put your hands on me."

Her eyes open and the second they meet mine, something sparks between us, something fierce and powerful. Something that shuts the world out and creates a new kind of intimacy between us.

You need to be careful, dude.

She reaches out and closes her warm palm over my dick, rubbing the way I taught her the last time we got naked. Was that only yesterday?

"Open your mouth," I command in a firm tone, and I don't miss the visible quiver that goes through her. She parts her lips, and swipes her tongue over her soft pink lips, and I swear to God, it's all I can do not to immediately shoot down her throat.

I step up to her, and tap my crown on the crook in her upper lip. "Do you think this pretty mouth can take my cock?"

"I'll do my best."

"If I want to shove it down your throat, will you do your best to take me?"

She swallows, her eyes a bit wide as she takes my dick into her hand and weighs it. "Yes."

"What if I shoot off a load, Anna? Will you do your best to swallow every last drop?"

"I will," she says, and my pulse pounds. I'm pretty sure I've never wanted or needed anyone or anything like I need her right now. "I want that, Alek."

I place my cock between her lips and she widens her jaw. I go slow, inching forward, and catching me by surprise she moves, taking me to the back of her throat. She gags, and her eyes water as I cut off her air supply. I instantly try to pull out, but she doesn't let me. No, she keeps me in her mouth, wanting the sensations. My heart squeezes tight. Dammit, I want to give this girl everything she needs.

She finally inches back and I pull almost all the way out, and she licks my crown. I touch her hair, move it from her face, and she glances up at me, waiting for me to do something.

"Fuck me with your mouth," I say, knowing that's what she wants. She moves her head back and forth, her wet saliva coating my aching dick. She's gorgeous taking me in like this, and her soft moans of enjoyment, they tug at something deep inside me, something long ago buried, and never allowed to surface.

My dick swells even more, and she licks the pre-cum and moans like she's enjoying a popsicle treat. Every muscle in my body tenses in warning but no way is she going to get me off before I get her off. Not only that, if I don't touch her, taste her in the next ten seconds, I might spontaneously combust, and that just won't do. Not when we have so much experimenting to do while she's living with me.

I inch back and my dick falls from her swollen lips. She blinks up at me, a pout on her face. "What are you doing?" She reaches for my cock, and I jerk back. "Was I not doing it right? I can go faster, or slower. Just tell me."

Oh Christ.

"You were perfect. Everything you do is perfect. Watching my cock slide in and out of your pretty mouth…" I shake my head. "I was so close to coming, and I'm not ready for that yet, babe."

"But that's what I want. You asked if I'd swallow every last drop. Are you not going—"

"You'll get my cock, and you'll get every last drop of my cum, but first, I need my mouth on this hot, sweet pussy."

"Okay. But you promise I can have your cock back in my mouth."

Lord, does she have any idea what she's doing to me?

"I promise."

"Good, because I really liked sucking your cock, Alek."

"Yeah," is all I can answer, because I really liked it a lot too. Just like I like her a lot.

I'm not even going to put my cock into her tonight, but everything tells me I'm the one who's going to be fucked come morning.

ANNA

I lick my lips, tasting Alek on my tongue, thrilled that it won't be the last time he's in my mouth tonight. He'd better keep his promise and let me suck him again, otherwise... Otherwise what? A laugh bubbles in my throat. I have no power here. Okay, maybe that's not entirely true. I do seem to have power over this man where my body is involved. I love the way he wants me. It's exciting, thrilling, and empowering.

Seriously though, he's turning me into a sex maniac. I can't seem to stop thinking about his body, his touch, and touching him. I've never felt so free or had so much fun. I really should have been having sex all these years. Although I can't imagine it would be this exciting with just anyone, and I hate to admit it but when this is over, I think I'm going to miss him.

I push back my thoughts as Alek kicks off his shorts and stands before me totally naked. He is a work of art, sculpted by the most beautiful hands and I am the luckiest girl in the world to have this unobstructed view.

He pushes on my shoulders until I'm on my back, and he grips my panties and breathes in my scent as he slowly lowers them down my legs. His lips find my inner thighs and he presses hot wet, open-mouthed kisses, and the sensation travels upward and spreads through my core.

Once he has me completely free of clothes, he grips my thighs and widens them, putting my quivering pussy on display. He growls, and his muscles ripple, and he seems like he's holding something back. But dammit, I want him as wild and unraveled as I am.

"Touch me, Alek. Put your fingers inside me and eat my pussy."

"Christ girl, do you have any idea what it does to me when you say things like that?" He glances at me, and I blink at him with every ounce of innocence inside me. He shakes his head. "Yeah, you do know."

He lightly strokes me, going from the top of my clit to my opening. Those big strong hands touch me with such gentleness it raises my temperature from normal to inferno in seconds. He pushes a finger into me, and I whimper as he stretches me. God, it's so gloriously delicious, my body wants to give in to the pleasure, but I want this to last a little longer. The sooner I come, the sooner I get his cock back, though.

"I have so much to do to get this hot pussy ready for me."

"I'm sorry," I murmur, hoping I'm not disappointing him with my innocence. Maybe he's not enjoying the prolonged foreplay.

His deep rich laugh rumbles around me. "Sorry? Oh, baby, I couldn't ask for anything more, and really, I don't even deserve this." He leans in and licks my clit. My hips come off the bed. "Taking my time with you might be hard, but I'm enjoying every fucking moment of it."

"My inexperience isn't...offputting?"

"It's the complete opposite." He takes his dick in his hand. "Do you see what you do to me?"

I chuckle like a silly schoolgirl, and he just shakes his head at me. "I'm so glad you didn't let your father marry you off."

I resist the urge to tell him I'm in hiding because he's still trying. I lift my hips and bump his face. He chuckles against my not-so-subtle hint. "Such a needy, needy girl."

He eats at my clit, sucks on it and nibbles it between his teeth. A moan curls around me, and I love that he loves what he's doing. I writhe and buck as my clit swells beneath his ministrations. I wrap my hands around his head and hold him to me. He lets me, but then he pulls away, leaving cold where there was once heat.

"Please..." I beg.

"Babe, we have so many other things to do tonight."

"This is all I want to do," I say bluntly, honestly. No sense in hiding what he does to me. My body hides no secrets.

He pulls out from between my legs, and I whimper my disapproval. He chuckles at my neediness, but I don't care, and you know what? I don't think he's as in control as he's letting on either. A creaking noise fills the room and I turn as he pulls open the top drawer on his nightstand.

"I did something," he murmurs.

I go up on my elbows to see what he's talking about, and my eyes go wide and my heartbeat speeds up when he pulls out a bunch of sex toys.

"I washed them all and put them in here for tonight."

"This…this was what you had delivered earlier."

"Yeah." He picks up a purple vibrator, adjusts the shape, and presses a button. It buzzes, and the end vibrates.

"Ohmigod, are you going to put that in me?"

"If you're afraid of this, babe, you're never going to be able to take my cock."

My body quivers with excitement. "I never said I was afraid."

"No?"

He grins, as I lay back, bend my knees and spread them wide. He takes the vibrator and circles my clit with it. "Ohmigod, Alek!"

He laughs. "Not what you were expecting?"

"Not really."

"This one is called Mr. Right." He rubs Mr. Right over my clit, changing the direction and pressure until I'm seeing freaking stars. Why does a man's penis not vibrate like this? It's glorious.

As he works my clit with the device, he grabs another, and I take in the long slick, dildo as he turns it on and it too begins to vibrate. He puts it on my nipples, his gaze latched on mine as he stimulates my puckered buds. The sensations rocket through me, and centers on my sex. He slides the vibrator down my body, and moves it to my opening. It's slender, like a tampon, and I'm glad. I don't want him to stretch me with any toy with more girth than he has. I want him to break my hymen with his cock, not a toy.

He inches it in, keeping an eye on me. I moan and grip the bedding, squeezing as he ever so slowly fills me and stimulates my clit at the same time. It's almost too much, yet not enough. That makes no sense, but I can't really think about anything other than the pleasure building in my body until nothing exists but this man manipulating the toy between my legs.

I grow wetter, lubricating the vibrator as he fucks me with it. I rock into it, barely able to get my breath. I try to talk, to moan, but no sound comes out when I open my mouth. Alek presses another button which changes the intensity on the slim vibrator.

"That's it. Take it all, Anna. Take this vibrator into your hot, tight cunt. Show me that you can handle every inch, and once you do, I'll ruin you with my cock like you want."

His dirty words do the most ridiculous things to me. "Alek," I practically scream as an orgasm builds and builds, severe pleasure spreading through me, until I break beneath him. "Yes."

"That's it," he murmurs. "Come all over your vibrator, like the good girl you are."

He eases off my clit, but keeps the other toy inside me as one hard wave after another grips my core, and I curl into myself as I ride them out. My body finally stops vibrating, and I gasp for air. Was I even breathing? I'm pretty sure I wasn't.

He slowly removes the vibrator and turns them both off. His grin is soft and warm as he lightly caresses my deliciously used sex.

"Alek," I finally manage to get out as he climbs up my body, his lips finding mine. I slide my arms around his moist body and hold him to me. We kiss deeply, breathe heavily into each other's mouth as the world spins around me.

"I didn't hurt you, did I?"

"Not at all." I touch his face, loving how sweet and thoughtful he is, and in my heart, I get the sense this man would never purposely hurt me. Trust is such a hard thing for me, and while I want to be careful and cautious, there's a part of me that is opening up to him.

His cock throbs against my leg, and another rush of excitement wells up inside me. I push on his chest with both hands. Unfortunately, he's too big and too strong and I can't move him an inch.

"Are you pushing me off you, Anna?"

"I'm trying."

He angles his head, a measure of worry in his eyes. "Are you okay?"

"No."

He stiffens, and rolls off me. "What's wrong?"

Once he's on his side, and a little off balance, I'm able to maneuver him until he's flat on his back. I crawl between his legs and take his dick in my hand. "What's wrong is your cock is in desperate need of my attention."

"Ah, yes. You might be right about that." He reaches out, and brushes my hair from my face, and it occurs to me how much he likes watching me take him deep. I turn my attention to his crown, to the pre-cum pooling on the end. I dip into it, and he groans as I use it to lubricate him.

I glance at him. "When do you think I'll be ready for you to fuck me?"

"Christ, Anna. Keep talking like that and I'll flip you over and fuck you hard."

"Okay then. Do you think my tight little pussy is going to be able to take your fat cock?"

"You're a tease, you know that, right?' He shakes his head and opens his mouth again, but I chuckle, bend forward and take him into my mouth. Whatever he was going to say is now lost on a groan. I taste him with my tongue, run the tip along his swollen veins, and cradle his balls in my palm. I pay attention to the noises he makes, understanding what he likes and what he doesn't, although he appears to like everything I do to him.

He grips my hair and I relax my throat, waiting to take his cock. It was a mix of pain and pleasure, and I honestly didn't even care that I couldn't get air. I wanted to do that for him. I rock against him and his hand moves with the motion of my head, and I go deeper, and deeper, surprising even myself as his grunts and curses urge me on. I pull back, lick him some more and run one hand up and down his thick shaft.

"You're killing me, babe." His voice is raspy, broken, strained, and it drives up the need building inside me. I'm not sure when he's finally going to put this gorgeous cock inside me, but I can't wait.

He grips my hair, as he swells in my mouth, and he tugs, but no way am I budging. I moan in protest around his cock.

"Are you sure?" he asks.

I nod, and fuck him with my mouth. Sucking and licking and coaxing his orgasm. "Anna. I'm going to come." Warm liquid fills my mouth as he spurts into it, and I swallow as he fills me up, taking in every last tangy drop. He grunts and curses and cups the side of my face as I let him deplete himself.

"Babe," he whispers when his cock stops spasming, and I lift my face. His eyes are dark, intense, full of warmth and appreciation. I grin at him.

"That was fun."

He laughs. "Yeah, babe, that was fun. Come here." He pulls me to him, until I'm lying over his body, his strong heartbeat against my cheek. I melt into him, a huge, contented smile on my face.

I chuckle, and he shifts. "Um, I don't really appreciate a girl laughing after sex."

I whack him. "Oh, you and your ego. Wait, do many women laugh at you after sex?"

"Not that I remember."

I fight off the stupid wave of jealousy, place my hands on his chest, and rest my chin on them so I can see him. "I wasn't laughing at you. I was just thinking, you might have won the wager—sort of," I say and give him a wink. "But I think I was the winner tonight."

He leans forward and drops a tender kiss onto my forehead. "No babe, I was the winner. Trust me on that."

There's that word trust again, and truthfully, hearing him say that fills me with an unfamiliar warmth, one that encourages me to forget logical reason and give a little more of myself to him. My heart thumps harder in my chest, things I shouldn't be feeling tapping at the door. But giving myself over to them would be a huge mistake. I can't stay here, not that he's asking me to, and while he might be strong and powerful, there's no way he could stand up to my family. Even if he wanted to, I couldn't let him. They have plans for me that don't involve Alek Hail.

I can't ever forget that.

12

ALEK

Once everyone is loaded into the SUV, and all our things for the cottage are packed, I brace my hands on the hatch. I can't really afford a week away from the office, and I'll have to do some work from the cottage, but I think we could all use a bit of down time. I secure the suitcases, the coolers, the groceries, and toss Anna's bag in.

"Did you bring everything you own?" I ask as I place her bag on top of mine, a bag I recently carried from our neighbors' house to mine.

"Yes, I think so."

I laugh at that. "Are you planning a quick getaway?" Her face pales slightly, and my insides go cold. The more time I spend with her, the more I'm convinced she's on the run. Her parents might want her to get married, old fashioned as they are, but that wouldn't be a reason to flee, right? I stare at her as she stares back. "Anna?"

She blinks and pulls herself together. "No, I just don't have a whole lot, and I like to keep my things close."

I close the hatch, walk around to the driver's side and slide in. Christ, I wish she felt safe with me. Maybe if I told her who I really was, and that my powerful family wouldn't let anything happen to her, it might ease her worries. Not only that, I can stand on my own two feet and protect her. If she doesn't want to get married, no one is going to force her. If they try, they'll have to go through me, and good fucking luck with that.

"Do you need to call anyone, to let them know you'll be away for a few days?"

She swallows. "No, it's okay."

Is she really this alone in the world? Possession and protectiveness claw to the surface like an angry bear guarding its cub. I reach across the seat and capture her hand. Like her, I don't always see eye to eye with my family, but they have my back, in good times and in bad, and I also have Chase.

Speaking of Chase, I glance at him in the rear-view mirror and as we make eye contact, he once again starts asking for a turtle. "I told you I'd think about it." I turn back to Anna. "You still don't have a bathing suit, do you?"

"No, but I should be fine."

I laugh. "Yeah, I won't be. I have an idea."

"Oh." I back out of the driveway, shut the garage, and ease into traffic. "Where are we going?"

"My parents' place." Her fingers link on her lap. "I thought I'd drop Chase off for a bit, and you and I can go do some shopping."

"I don't really have any—"

"It's fine, Anna."

"No, it's not, actually. I might not be as *old* or as wise as you, but I've learned a thing or two over the years."

"Do tell."

"Nothing in life is free. You end up paying one way or another."

"I agree with that."

Her brows lift in surprise, then she nods. "Good, then you'll understand that I like to pay my own way in life."

A woman not looking for something from me. Isn't that a refreshing break? I smile at her, liking that very much about her.

"Why are you smiling at me like that?" she asks.

"Like what?"

"You're scaring me, Alek."

I laugh. "You know you have nothing to be afraid of when it comes to me, right?"

"I did, until you started smiling like the joker." She shifts in her seat and presses against the window and this playful side of her brings on a full belly laugh.

"I was just thinking." I lower my voice. "If we pick you up a couple of new suits, I'm sure we can find a way for you to pay me back."

She folds her arms and nods. "Oh, I see how it is."

"And..."

"I can get behind that," she says.

I grin, because yeah, I'm the one who's going to be getting behind that, and when I say that, I mean Anna. I'm going to take this gorgeous woman in all ways. My dick swells just thinking about it, but I talk him down. Nothing good can come from having a huge boner when I get to my parents' house.

We fall silent, and Chase plays with his video game as I drive. I reach the gate and she sits up a little straighter. "This is where your parents live?" She seems surprised by the luxury, and why wouldn't she be? All her worldly belongings fit into one duffle bag.

"Yeah," I say.

"We're at Grandma and Grandpa's!" Chase shouts.

"You want to hang out here for a bit, little man? Anna and I are going to do some shopping." He's already starting to unbuckle as the iron gate yawns open. "Sit tight for a second."

I drive through the gate, and I'm grateful the guard isn't standing by the door when I stop the vehicle. How would I have explained that without giving away who I really am?

Chase jumps from the car, and Anna sits there, uncertainty in her eyes. Maybe all the wealth makes her uncomfortable. "I'll just be a second, okay?"

She visibly relaxes, happy that she doesn't have to come inside. "Okay." She shakes her phone. "I have to check my messages anyway."

I often hear her phone ring, but she never answers it. "I'll be fast."

I hurry inside, and Mom and Dad are already hugging and fussing over Chase.

"Chase says you're going to the cottage?" Mom says, delight in her eyes. She touches my cheek. "You work too hard, Alek. I'm happy to see you taking a break. Will you be going alone?"

"No, uh, Chase's nanny is coming." My parents would consider her hiding in the car disrespectful, but I didn't want to bring her inside. One look at us and they'd no doubt know we were fucking, and of course she's so young. I don't need the lecture today, and that would likely prompt them to push me harder into marriage. I jerk my thumb over my shoulder. "She wanted to meet you, but she had an emergency call to take."

I'm sure Dad is about to say something, but Chase pipes in and asks his grandparents if he can have a turtle.

"Of course, you can, Chase," Dad says, and I roll my eyes. I should have known this was coming. If Dad doesn't buy it, just ask Grandpa.

"No turtles, Dad."

My father meets my gaze. "We'll discuss this later."

"I have some things I need to pick up for the week away. I'll be back in a couple of hours. I really appreciate you watching Chase on such short notice."

"Of course," Mom says, and I give her a kiss on the cheek before they lead him away. Back in the car, I glance at Anna, who gives me a smile and puts her phone away.

"Everything okay?"

"Everything is good," she says. "They didn't mind watching Chase?"

"No, they love him. They don't get to see him as much as they'd like, but everyone is busy."

"It's nice that you're so close."

I touch her hand, give it a squeeze. "I'm sorry you're not close to your family."

"I am. But I just want to live a different life than the one they want for me."

"Kind of the same as me. I guess we have more in common than we realize."

I drive around the circular driveway, exit through the gate and it closes behind us.

"They have some security here."

"Yeah," I agree. I don't bother telling her that we probably have a tail. Hell, Dad's guards likely knew who Anna was the second our hands touched in the apple bin. I steal a glance at her, take in her pallor, and her cheekbones. She's been eating well since we met, and I'm happy about that. But she does need clothes that fit.

I drive to the shopping district. "I'm not much into women's stores, so let me know which ones you like."

She goes quiet, like she doesn't know either, and I wonder who's been picking out her clothes all these years. "That one there looks good." She points to a lingerie store. "I think it might be a bit pricey though."

"Good, then I can make you pay in all kinds of fun ways."

She grins, as I ease my car into a parking spot. "I won't be long."

I unbuckle. "I'm coming with you."

"I'm perfectly capable of picking out a bathing suit, Alek."

"You did have trouble with watermelon, so if you run into any problems, I want to be there to help."

She eyes me. "Maybe you're just hoping to get a glimpse of all the pretty girls in their bathing suits."

"The only pretty girl I want to see in a bathing suit is you, Anna." She blinks at me, warmth and appreciation in her eyes. Jesus, this woman hasn't been told enough how incredible she is, how she should be worshiped on a daily basis.

"Okay," she concedes softly, and looks up and down the sidewalk before she jumps from the car and darts into the store before I can even catch up to her. What, does she not want to be seen with me? Inside, the scent of warm vanilla washes over me, and there are only a few customers inside, making it easy for me to find Anna, who is looking through a rack of swim suits.

"Find anything?" I ask as I step up behind her and her body quivers as my breath washes over the back of her neck.

"I think so." She pulls a pretty two-piece from the rack and shows it to me. "Do you like it?"

"I'll let you know after I see it on you."

"I don't really want to try things on." She backs up a bit as a woman walks by. "We can just get this. I'm sure it's my size and we don't want to keep Chase waiting."

"Chase is having the time of his life at my folks' house. Don't worry about it." After noting the size of the suit in Anna's hand, I move to another section of the store where the designer suits are displayed. I flick through the suits, and pull out a couple different styles. "What do you think of these?"

She checks the tags and cringes. "They're a bit pricey."

"That wasn't what I asked."

She puckers her lips and glares at me. "They're nice. But I have this one."

"You'll need more than one suit at the cottage."

"I don't really—"

I pile them into her hand. "Go try them on."

She opens her mouth and I shake my head to stop her.

"Fine." She walks to the back of the store, and my gaze is on her sweet ass tucked into a pair of jean shorts. They're not cheap shorts. No, she might not have a lot of clothes with her, but her clothes are quality.

As she changes into the first one, I take a look at bathing suit cover ups, and find some summer dresses that would look nice on her. I have my arms full by the time she calls out to me.

"I'm here."

"I don't want to come out."

"Do you like it?"

"I do," she says, and I put my hand on the curtain, and move it a bit so I can peek in. She yelps when she sees me in the mirror. "What are you doing?"

"It's okay if you don't want to come out, but I'm coming in." My gaze leaves her face, trails down her thin, tanned body, and my cock swells. Curses rumble in my throat.

"You don't like it?" she asks, her shoulders sagging slightly.

"I love it, and if I thought we could be quiet, I'd come in and fuck you right here, up against the mirror."

Heat moves into her cheeks, and she makes a little whimpering sound. I grin. She likes the idea of that, but when I finally take her, it will be in private where she's completely comfortable to call out, or even scream my name. Yeah, I plan to make her sing gospel when I put my dick in her.

"Here." I hand over the cover ups and dresses. "Try these on too." I stand there, my head inside her curtain.

"Aren't you going to leave?"

"Are you afraid I'm going to see something I've never seen before?"

"Get out," she says, and I laugh.

"Fine. But I'm right here so let me know after you put the next thing on."

For the next twenty minutes, she tries everything on, and except for two items, we're taking it all. She changes back into her jean shorts and T-shirt and her hair is a wild mess when she steps from the change room. She never looked more adorable.

"Can we get Chase and go to the cottage now?"

"Yup, unless you want to hit any more stores."

"I think we've done enough damage here." We walk up to the counter, and the door opens. A woman rushes up to the counter and drops her purse.

"I'm sorry I'm late, Cassandra," she blurts out, and hops behind the counter and starts folding all the clothes and bagging them. "Traffic was crazy."

I pull my wallet from my pocket, and the girl glances at me, her smile turning flirtatious as she inches closer. "Hi there. Is there anything I can help you with?"

"No, we're all set." Why the hell is she flirting with me when Anna is right beside me? I turn to Anna, but she's tucked in behind me, out of view, like she's trying to make herself invisible. What the hell is going on. "Anna?"

"I think I have something in my eye. I'll head outside."

She steps around me, and the flirtatious girl shrieks, comes out from behind the counter and grabs Anna by the shoulder. My entire body stiffens, and I don't know why, but images of my best friend getting shot in the crossfire and dying on the way to the hospital flash before my eyes. Perhaps it's because everything about Anna, from her body language to the strange way she's acting—like her fight or flight instincts are kicking in, and in this case I think it's flight—sends warning signals to my brain.

I'm about to move Anna and stand between them when Anna lifts her head, and plasters on a smile, as fake as a smile can get. "Chloe, hey so nice to see you." She's blinking rapidly, her breath coming fast as she greets her friend. "I didn't realize that was you."

Chloe's gaze slides to me. "Wow, it looks like your situation has improved."

"Excuse me?" Confused, my gaze goes back and forth between Anna and Chloe.

"Oh, this is Alek. A friend of mine. Alek, this is Chloe. We went to high school together. We're just headed out. We're in a hurry. Nice to see you, Chloe. Let's catch up soon, okay?"

Chloe playfully winks at Anna. "Yeah, if my bodyguard looked like that, I'd want to hurry home and try all these on for him too."

A moan of mortification crawls out of Anna's throat. But Chloe's face softens and she touches Anna's arm. "Can I talk to you for a second?"

"I can't. I do have to run. Soon, though."

I snatch up the bag and follow her out. "What the hell was that all about?" I ask. "What did she mean by bodyguard?"

She shakes her head. "Chloe was a mean girl. A lot of people needed protection from her."

My body tenses. "Did you?"

"I had...friends. So, she didn't really mess with me too much."

"These friends. They were like bodyguards."

"Something like that." She hurries to the SUV, and I hit the fob because she looks like she's desperate to get inside.

I head to the back of the vehicle, but when the hairs on my nape begin to tingle, I can't help but glance up and down the street. Someone is watching, of that much, I'm sure. Not that I'd ever be able to identify the person. No, my father hires the best of the best.

Trying to shake off the uneasy feeling that always resides within me, I toss the bags into the back and slide into the driver's seat. I want to ask more questions, but Anna looks like she's seen a ghost. Maybe it's best to let her past stay in the past, and maybe this trip to the cottage will be the best thing for her. Maybe she'll relax a bit, let her guard down.

"I think we've got everything you needed," I say, letting her know Chloe will not be discussed further.

Her shoulders relax and this time her smile is genuine. "I do too." She crinkles her nose.

"What?" I ask.

"This is going to cost me a lot, isn't it?"

No, it's not going to cost her a thing, but she's a girl who wants to pay her way, and I don't want to make her feel less than the incredible woman she is, so I wiggle my eyebrows and grin. "Big time."

13

——

ANNA

——

I take deep breaths, unable to believe my run-in with Chloe. I wasn't lying when I said she was a mean girl. She teased and tormented me about always having a bodyguard in the near vicinity. Normally we couldn't see them, but we all knew one was there. My heart starts to settle as Alek lets the conversation go, and I'm grateful he's not pressing. I just want to go away this weekend and have a nice time at his lakeside hideout, where I don't have to keep looking over my shoulder. I can't remember the last time I was able to relax and let go.

I remain quiet as we drive back to his parents' place to pick up Chase and every now and then, I feel his eyes on me. We reach his parents' estate, and the gate opens for us. After he parks, he casts me a glance and I pull my phone from my pocket, pretending I have more messages to answer.

"I'll just be a sec, okay."

I nod. It's not like I'm anxious to meet his parents, and it's clear he doesn't want me to, otherwise he would have invited me in when we were here earlier. Maybe he thinks they'll interrogate me or something. Sitting here is all for the best. The fewer people who know me the better, and I'll be getting out of Dodge soon enough.

I scroll through my phone, and my finger hovers over the screen. Should I respond to my parents? I had numerous messages from them, and while I did once tell them I was okay—not to worry about me—I'm not sure if I should send any more messages.

Alek comes back with Chase and he's excited as he climbs into the car, and from around the corner, I spot a man standing there watching us, his gaze alert, and the hairs on my neck tingle in warning. I know that stance, that look.

"Is that your father?" I ask.

"No, just a friend of the family."

He doesn't elaborate, and I don't push it. I guess we all have our own secrets. Chase talks about his grandfather buying him a turtle and Alek just rolls his eyes at me.

"My parents spoil him."

"That's good." I turn to smile at Chase and as I take in his features, my heart squeezes. He looks so much like his father. Once again, I wonder about his mother but I don't ask. "Kids should be spoiled by their grandparents," I say.

He laughs. "Yeah, you say that now. Wait until you have kids of your own, and you start losing control."

While I'm not the girlie girl who dreams of big weddings, I have given some thought to having kids of my own. "I'm not planning on having kids."

His gaze jerks to mine. "Oh, that surprises me."

"Why is that?"

He checks his side mirror before passing a slow vehicle as he turns onto the highway. "You're so good with Chase, and with Sophie."

I nod. "I didn't say I didn't like kids. I just don't plan to have any."

He nods, but his brow is furrowed. Obviously, he doesn't understand my life—and why would he, I haven't shared much about my life, or why I don't want to bring kids into this world, considering what my family does for a living. They'd want to control them every bit as much as they want to control me. And there's the danger of being kidnapped or killed by rival gangs.

"You're still young." He shrugs. "Things change, life changes, circumstances change, but I get it. Right now, you have a lot of things you want to do, and you should do them."

"Thanks." I smile at him, and wish my family was as understanding as he was.

Chase pipes up from the back seat, talking about how he wants to go fishing and out on the boat, and he wants to finally learn how to water ski.

"How about we just tie the floaty to the back of the jet ski."

"Do you water ski?" I ask him.

"I do, and Chase is determined to learn, but he's too young."

I laugh. "He's too young and I'm too old."

"No, you're not. If you want to learn, I can teach you."

"I'd break my neck."

This time he laughs. "No, you won't. But if you want to try, I can teach you."

"I don't know. We'll see." My phone rings, and he glances at me.

"Are you going to get that?"

"Nope, vacation has officially started. Well, vacation for you, not me. You did mention that you had a to-do jar at the cottage. But still, no phone for me this week." He grins at me, and even though I haven't known him long, and he's rigid about most things, he does seem to have relaxed a tiny bit. This vacation will be good for him, and I plan to make sure he has a relaxing time. I just hope there's some fun things in the to-do jar.

I quietly sing along to the radio, and I don't even care that I have a horrible voice, or that every now and then I turn to find Alek smirking at me. It prompts me to sing louder, and when he joins in, Chase laughs from the back seat. Honestly, when was the last time I felt this much joy?

We chat about the weather, last year's hockey season—he's a big Blackhawks fan and is determined to turn me into one— and he mentions the repairs he'd like to do this week at the cottage, and I like that he's a rich, successful educated man who isn't afraid of hard work.

Hours later, we make it to a long dirt road, and he eases off the main road, and slows. I glance at all the cottages dotting the lake as we drive, and excitement wells up inside me as I wait to see which one we're going to pull into.

He finally takes a turn down a long winding driveway and when his cottage comes into view, a huge smile splits my lips. "It's gorgeous, Alek."

"Let me out, let me out," Chase says from the back seat, and the second Alek puts the car into park, Chase jumps out. I climb from the passenger seat and breathe in the fresh clean air, and a calmness washes over me as the waves lap against the dock.

"Not too close," Alek calls out to Chase as he heads to the shore. "He's a great swimmer. I started him in lessons early because of the pool."

"You're a good dad." I turn to watch Chase.

Alek's energy reaches out to me as he steps closer, and he puts his big hands on my arms, and rubs gently. "You're not as tightly wound as you were when I first met you."

"I think the cottage is going to be good for me." I lean against him, rest the back of my head on his chest, and his strong heartbeat brings on a sense of security and comfort. "How long have you had this place?"

"I got it when..."

His voice falls off, and I instantly know he was about to talk about Chase's mother. "It's okay."

His mouth is near my ear, his breath warm on my neck as he speaks. "Chase's mother wanted a cottage. We got this for her. Chase likes it, so I don't want to sell it."

"Is it hard being here?" I push off him, and turn to face him. He looks over my head at his son before he dips his head to see me.

"I don't love her. Not anymore. But she'll always be Chase's mother, and we did have good times together. I try to remember that when I'm here. I try to remember that it wasn't all bad. Chase was made out of love."

My heart beats a little faster, and as it does, the craziest thing begins to happen. It opens a bit, allows foreign emotions in—things I don't want to feel for this man. He's my boss. I'm his employee. We're having sex, but there's no room for more in this messed up relationship. Heck, he didn't even want to introduce me to his family, and I didn't want to meet them. I close my eyes and mentally pull myself together.

"That's a great attitude to have. Especially for Chase. It's not easy for you, being a mother and a father."

He goes quiet for so long, I think the conversation is over, but then he says quietly, "She just up and left one day." Sadness invades his eyes, and they narrow, hurt all over his face. "Who does that?"

"I don't know," I answer quietly, and I really don't. "I have no idea how a mother could leave her child behind."

"I don't even really care that she cleaned out the safety deposit box, and drained most of our joint account. I care about how it hurt Chase. I couldn't bring myself to tell him that she just walked away. I didn't want him to hurt more than he already was. I didn't want him to hate her."

She cleaned him out!

"I'm so sorry she did that to you, Alek." I put my arms around him, and give him a hug. "I know people use their kids as pawns in lots of situations and it shows me how sweet you are to protect Chase from her behavior and not to speak unkindly of her." I lift my head and place my chin on his chest. "I had a boyfriend just up and leave too. We didn't date long, though. It's not your situation, but I can maybe understand a bit of how you felt." I'm pretty sure my father scared him off and sent him to another state. A cold shiver moves through me. If he so much as lays a hand on Alek or Chase,

I'll go ballistic. I shouldn't have gotten involved, but it's too late for that now. I'll just have to be extra careful when in public.

"Are you cold?" he rubs my arms, mistaking the shiver.

"There was a breeze."

He fishes a key from his pocket and hands it to me. "Go inside and get settled." I'm about to oblige, but he stops me. "I don't know why I told you all that."

"It's because you're here, and there's still rawness to it all." I put my hand over his heart. "In here."

His hand closes over mine. "My problems aren't your problems, though."

"How about this? While we're here, we forget our problems, but if we want to talk about them, we can, no judgement."

"I like that." He offers me an adorable smile. "Thanks for listening."

"Anytime."

"There are two spare bedrooms. Pick whichever one you want."

I nod. Of course, we won't be sharing a room. We don't want to send the wrong message to Chase. He opens the trunk, and pulls out our bags. "You said you never brought any employees here before?

He shrugs like it's nothing. "Never wanted to."

I arch my brow in question. "And now you do because you want to make some new memories?"

"I'm not even sure I knew that, but I think you're right." He touches my face, brushes his thumb over my bottom lip and his warmth careens through my body. "I like being with you, Anna, and there is no one else I'd rather make new memories with."

A wave of happiness careens through me, giving me all the feels, all the things I shouldn't be feeling. "I like being with you too, and I'm happy to help you make new memories of the cabin. Better ones." I glance out and spot Chase standing in the shallow water. "On the lake, in the boat...in the bedroom."

"Now that's an offer I'll never refuse." He grins at me. "Why don't you head inside, and I'll bring everything in."

"I'm not useless," I tell him, and walk to the back of the vehicle to load up.

"I've got this." His voice is a little deeper, a lot firmer and my body goes into hyper drive, loving his ridiculous take charge attitude.

"If you insist...sir."

I saunter off without any of the bags, and Chase comes running up to me. I open the door and he bursts inside. The place is rustic and warm, and I love it completely. "Which room is yours, Chase?"

I follow him down a long hall and he dashes to his room and flops on his bed. "At night, when the lights are out, you can see the stars." I glance up to see white stickers in the shape of stars on his ceiling.

"How lovely. Which room do you think I should take?"

He jumps from his bed, and I follow him. In the next room, he throws himself onto a big king-sized bed, and I'm pretty sure I'm in Alek's master suite.

"This is your father's room. I need my own."

He frowns, throws his feet over the edge, and puts his hands on his knees, so serious, I bite back a laugh. "Yeah, but if you sleep in here, you could be my new mommy," he says so dead-pan, I'm sure he must be cracking a joke.

"Chase?"

"Grandpa said Dad is getting a new wife, which means I'm getting a new mommy, and I don't know if I'll like her or if she'll like me. I like you, Anna, so can't you just be my new mommy?"

Footsteps behind me come to a resounding halt, and I don't need to turn to know Alek is standing there, and undoubtedly heard Chase's plea.

Kill me freaking now.

My anger flares as I stand back and listen to my son ask Anna if she'll be his mother. Not because I hate what he's asking, but because my parents put that ridiculous idea into his head when they had no right to even broach the subject with him. How dare they overstep and talk about adult matters that he shouldn't be worrying about? Christ, I love my folks, and they love Chase, but where is their common sense? Why on earth would they tell him he's getting a new mommy? I told them I'd think about it. That wasn't confirmation and Chase has been through enough already and doesn't need something else to stress over.

I take two fast breaths to calm myself down as Anna slowly turns my way. Her eyes are big, apologetic, and she mouths the word, *sorry*.

"You don't have anything to be sorry about," I tell her as I move closer, until her body is a hairbreadth away from mine. I like being close to her like this. Maybe it feels like we're a team here, a united force where Chase is concerned. Where life is concerned. But that's also a crazy thought. Maybe I'm more like my parents than I realize.

"I don't know what to say."

I nod, and lightly brush her knuckles. "I'll deal with it." I lift my head and gesture with a nod to the room across the hall. "You go get settled." She nods and walks off and when her door quietly shuts behind her, I walk across the room and plunk down beside Chase.

"Hey bud, I heard what you asked Anna."

He plucks at the bedding, clearly distressed, and I choke back my anger to present a calm façade to my precious son. "Can she be my new mommy?" he asks.

I give him a smile, and shift closer. "It's not as simple as that, I'm afraid."

"Why not?" His voice is a little wobbly as he turns on the bed, and sits cross-legged.

I ruffle his hair as worried eyes stare up at me and my heart squeezes so tight, it's almost impossible to breathe. "I don't want you to worry about a new mommy, but if I ever find you a new mommy, I promise I will check with you, so we both will know that she's nice, and fun and that we'll love being with her, okay?" I pick him up and put him on my lap. "I would never, ever bring anyone into the house if you didn't like her. You remember Hilda, right?"

"She was mean."

"She just had her own way of doing things, but I knew you didn't like her, so she didn't stay."

He puts his arms around me, and my throat tightens to the point of pain. "I like the way you do things, Daddy."

"I'm glad."

"I like the way Anna does things too. She's nice and fun and I love playing with her."

"I do too, buddy."

Oh, do I ever like playing with her.

"She's nice, isn't she?" I say absentmindedly, a small smile on my face as my heart speeds up a bit, spreading warmth and other things I probably shouldn't be feeling through my body.

He bounces on my leg and says, "Yeah."

I pick him up and set him on the floor. "What do you say we go see if she wants to go out on the boat?"

"Are we going water skiing?"

I laugh. "You're like a dog with a bone, Chase."

His eyes go big. "Are we getting a dog?"

"No, we're getting a turtle, remember." Shit. What am I saying? I really have a hard time saying no to him, but maybe he does need a pet. A turtle must be less work than a dog, and well, I have bad memories of losing my dog. He just disappeared one day, and I was told he went to go live on a farm. Now I understand what that means, and I'm pretty sure Sam, my three-year-old lab, didn't die of old age. I cringe to think what might have happened to him. "When we get back, we can all go to the pet store, okay?"

"Yay," he screeches and rushes out of the room just as Anna opens her bedroom door, and comes out in a pair of frayed shorts and a T-shirt. Her face is shiny clean, her hair pulled back. She's never looked prettier.

"We're getting a turtle." I grumble and shake my head.

She smiles at me, and it's full of warmth and love.... Okay, maybe not love, but more like sweetness and vulnerability. "I had no doubt. Deep in here"—She touches my heart—"You're a real softie, aren't you?"

"No," I grouch and put on a stern face, but it does nothing to wipe the sweet smile from her face.

"Ah, too bad. I really like a guy who's a softie at heart."

"Okay, well maybe I am." What the fuck am I saying? It's not like I want her to like me, like that. Maybe I do and maybe I have a damn brain tumor. Sure, I like what I know about her, but it boils down to this: I barely know her. I should not be letting my parents put ideas into my head through my son. "It's like this. I felt bad. Chase shouldn't have to worry about a new mommy and whether he'll like her or not."

"You're right." She frowns and glances down. "That's a lot to process and a new mother should not be thrust upon him." She shakes her head. "Your parents really want you married off that badly?"

I scrub my hand over my face. "I'll be having words with my parents. In their brains, they already have me married to some girl I've never met. I have no doubt Mom is planning some big bash in the backyard."

"Don't be too hard on them. I think they only have your and Chase's best interests at heart."

"I know, but still..."

"Maybe you'll like the girl they want to set you up with. Have you ever given that consideration?"

I arch a brow. "You're not going to like what I'm about to say in response to that, Anna."

She briefly closes her eyes, a grin on her face as she snorts. "Touché. I get it. Maybe I'll like the guy my parents are trying to force upon me. Truthfully, I'd never considered it before. I just have so much I want to do, and getting married at a young age isn't on that list."

Chase runs through the place, breaking the quiet moment. "Do you want to go out on the boat, or do you want to just relax inside for a bit and unpack?"

"Boat, please."

I laugh at that. "Let me get the food into the fridge and then boat it is." She follows me down the hall to the kitchen. "Chase, go get your suit on."

Chase goes back to his room, and Anna unloads the groceries and I put them away. "What a team."

She grins at me. "I should probably get changed too." She disappears and I go to my room and tug on some board shorts. Chase and I head outside, and I finish covering him in sunscreen as Anna comes out looking gorgeous in her new two-piece bikini. I toss her the lotion.

"You have life jackets, right?" She gazes out over the calm water. "I'm not the greatest swimmer."

"I've got everything."

Her gaze goes over my body, and she nibbles her lip, and I grin. Her eyes scream, *yeah, you got everything,* as she appraises me and I'm man enough to admit I like her eyes on me like that. She appreciates what she sees and the appreciation is mutual.

She lotions up and I try not to gawk as she rubs it over her long sleek legs. This is not the time for a boner.

"Come on, kiddo, let's get the life jackets."

After I get him fitted out, I toss mine into the boat, and hand Anna one. "You don't have to wear one if you don't want to."

"Yes, I do. Chase is probably a better swimmer than me."

I chuckle as she tugs it on, and I help her with the buckles. "This is a gorgeous boat," she says as she climbs on.

"I love being on the water." I take a breath, and my shoulders relax as I let it out. "There's just something so peaceful about it."

Anna nods. "No phone calls, no one to bother you. I can get behind that."

I untie us, push from the dock and start the motor. Chase is already messing with the fishing gear, and searching for the shiniest lure.

"I'm going to catch us dinner, Anna."

"That would be wonderful," she tells him as she sits down beside him. I steer the boat away from the dock, and listen in on their conversation as she asks Chase to teach her how to put her lure on the fishing line. Chase beams, and proceeds to show her and once I get the boat out to where I want it, I kill the motor.

"This is what you do, Anna," Chase says and stands. He whips the rod like I taught him, and Anna watches and learns. She mimics his motion perfectly. She's a fast learner. I like that.

"You're doing it," Chase praises her, so proud of his nanny, and I grin at the two as his earlier words bounce around inside my brain. *Can Anna be my new mommy?*

For the briefest of moments, I let my brain explore that idea. Anna making our small family of two a family of three, and then maybe four. Anna there for the holidays, for all the big events, and giving Chase all the female influence he needs. I shake that thought from my head because it's absolutely ludicrous. Anna doesn't want a family, and she has a lot to do before she will even think of settling down. I'm not the guy who is going to take that from her, but it does give me an idea, and I make a mental note to do a bit of research later, maybe make a few calls, and call in a few favors.

I drop down beside them and just sit and watch. She glances at me. "I think I'm using your rod. Do you want it back?"

"Nope, I'm happy to watch." It's not a lie. The smile on her face is just about the nicest thing I've seen in a long time. Chase reels his line in and Anna does the same.

She grins at me and wow, I really love this easy-going version of her. "Do you think I caught anything?"

"You'll feel a tug when you catch a fish, then you reel in." She finishes reeling all the way in and casts again.

"This is fun."

I laugh at her childlike enthusiasm. "I'm glad you're having fun."

Chase casts his line again, and bounces in his seat as he reels it in. The boat bobs in the lake and I lean back and let the sun warm my face. I'm glad Anna suggested coming here. I might have to work a bit while here, but it's so worth it.

After about five minutes of sitting back, Anna shrieks, and I jerk upright. "I think I caught something," she blurts out.

Chase starts clapping. "Reel it in slowly," he tells her, and she nods and does what he suggests.

"Well well, look at that." I rub my stomach. "What a feast we're going to have tonight." I laugh as I reach into the water and pull out a big stick.

"I caught a stick," she says and she doesn't seem upset by it at all. She laughs. "I caught a stick, and it's a mighty nice stick, too."

"You want to keep it?"

She gives me a look that suggests I might be insane. "Of course I do. I've never caught anything in my life, other than a cold. I'll have to put this in a showcase or something."

"Anna, you're funny," Chase says and starts laughing. We all join in and I set the stick down on the bottom of the boat.

I wag my brow at her. "I'm glad you're not going to make me cook it."

She sets the rod down. "Maybe we should head back in. It's hot out here. I'd love to have a swim."

"We don't need to go to the shore for that."

She frowns. "We don't?"

I stand and jump into the water, and Chase hurls himself in behind me. "Oh," she says, delight all over her face.

She steps up to the side of the boat and lands with a big splash. Her lifejacket keeps her at the surface. "It's cold," she screeches, her arms flailing, but she has the biggest smile on her face.

"You'll get used to it."

She waves her arms. "Actually, it's glorious." Flipping, she goes onto her back and stares at the clouds in the sky. "Look at that."

"What?"

I flip over and so does Chase. "That cloud looks like a turtle."

Chase laughs. "That one looks like a dog."

"Have you ever had a dog?" I ask her.

She frowns, and that sense of loss, loneliness is back on her face. It makes me want to pull her in, hug her to me and keep her safe forever.

"No, but I always wanted one."

"I was thinking about getting one." What the ever-loving fuck is happening to me. I don't want a dog.

But Anna does.

She straightens up and begins to tread water. "Really?"

"Yeah, really."

"We're getting a turtle and a dog," Chase screams and begins slapping the water.

"Yeah, we're getting a dog and a turtle," I say. I'm also getting a CAT scan because something is going on inside my brain. Either that or Anna is messing with me in ways that could be dangerous. I can't have that, which means when we get back to civilization, there is only one thing I can do.

Fire her.

ANNA

I finish setting the picnic table as Alek takes the trout off the grill. No, I didn't catch it, and neither did Chase. There's a cottage down the road and the owners stopped by after we anchored the boat and brought us a couple of trout they'd caught. It was incredibly nice of them, and we talked about getting together tomorrow night for dinner at their place. They even offered to take us out on their pontoon boat, which sounds like fun.

Since I've always been sheltered, treated like a child, it's really nice to be considered an adult, and I probably shouldn't like the idea of the neighbors thinking Alek and I are a couple quite so much. He didn't correct them, and neither did I. I guess out here in the middle of nowhere, we're living in some fantasy world, and while I normally deal in reality, I can't help but think at the lake—with Alek—it might be a safe place to explore a little fantasy. He's the only man in the world who makes me feel safe. I don't know why, I don't know how, I just know that he does and I'm going to enjoy every minute of it while I can.

I realize I told him that maybe he'd like the girl his parents want to set him up with, and he called me on my own arranged set up. Maybe I would like the guy, but seriously, on principle alone, I am not marrying some man I've never met and honestly I have a hard time believing my parents are putting my best interests first. I'm a pawn. Alek is in a different position, at a different stage of life. I can see why they would want a woman in his life, and a mother for Chase and see why they would want to help out considering his last relationship.

As I sort things over, I put a plate on each placemat, and scoop out some salad. Chase yawns and plunks down at the picnic table. He can barely keep his eyes open. All the fresh air is making me sleepy too.

"Tired?" I ask.

He fights a yawn and I bite back a smile. "No."

"I didn't think so." I glance up to see Alek grinning, and my entire body quivers just from being around him. My gaze moves past Alek to take in the gorgeous view as he turns the gas off on the barbecue. "Come here, Chase," I say, and he pushes from his seat and stumbles to my side of the table, his legs barely holding him up.

I put him on my lap. "Look at that." He gazes at the streaks of purple and pink bruising the evening sky. "Isn't that pretty?"

"Yeah," he says but this time he can't fight the yawn.

"Maybe tomorrow we could color that. Do you think that would be fun?"

He grins. "I like coloring."

"I know you do. I do too." I give him a kiss on the top of his head, my heart full.

He leans his head back on my shoulder, and I'm not sure what's happening inside my body, but this strange motherly instinct grips me. I've heard talk about a woman's biological clock, but I'm way too young for that, right? I make a mental note not to forget my birth control pills when Alek finally makes love to me, or rather fucks me. The birth control pill, combined with a condom, means there is no way in hell I'll get pregnant. That's the last thing in the world I want or need.

Is it, Anna?

"Hey," Alek says softly, and I lift my gaze to his. "Little man is sleeping."

I shift and look at Chase's face. His eyes are closed and his breathing has slowed. "My God, he's sweet when he's sleeping."

Alek puts the plate of food on the table, and scoops Chase up. Chase snuggles into him, his head resting on Alek's shoulder. "I'll put him to bed."

"What about his dinner?"

"He had that grilled cheese because he was *starving*, remember?" We both chuckle, because Chase can be dramatic at times. He acted like he was going to faint, forcing Alek to make him a sandwich. I shook my head at his antics. The kid really knows how to work his father. Alek loves it though, whether he wants to admit it or not and whether I want to admit it or not, I'm envious of what they have together.

I take a sip of my wine and stare at the sunset. For a second, I think about capturing the image with my phone, but instead decide to imprint it on my memory, just like I plan to do with this weekend. No photographic evidence, just warm memories to soothe my soul and keep me warm at night when our time is finished.

Alek comes back and sits beside me, instead of across from me, where I set his plate. He grabs the placemat and drags it to him, and I shift closer, needing his touch. He smiles at me, and stares at the sunset.

"Thanks."

"For what?" I ask.

"For being so sweet to Chase. I love that you showed him the sunset. I never would have thought to do that." He goes quiet, and puts a trout on each of our plates. "He does need a woman in his life." His big palm goes to my leg, and he gives it a light squeeze. "I'm glad he has you."

"He won't always though," I stupidly blurt out, and Alek stiffens. The movement is slight, but I still notice it. "I mean, I'll be going off to school as soon as I save up enough money." Jeez, am I pushing him toward this woman his parents have in mind? I don't know. It's possible, though. I want them both to have someone in their lives. Or maybe I'm pushing him to ask me to stay. God, I am such a mess right now. I want to experience life, but that means leaving Alek and Chase behind. But Alek isn't asking me to stay—of course he isn't, this is just sex—so I need to keep all these weird things I'm feeling under wraps.

He nods in agreement, and my stupid stomach sinks. Ah, what was that I just said about keeping my feelings under wraps.

"No, I get it, you're right."

I smile at him. "Until then, he has me." Alek looks away, his hand still lingering on my thigh. "You've got me too."

His gaze jerks back to mine, and a smile tugs at his mouth. "The question is, what am I going to do with you?"

With his mood once again playful, I stab a piece of cucumber and bring it to my mouth. I pretend I'm thinking as I chew. "Pretty much anything you want, I guess." A long pause and then, "Sir." He growls and a chuckle bubbles out of my throat. "Seriously, Alek. I love being here with you and Chase. It's like a whole other world."

He puts his hand on my shoulder and lightly massages. "I like the idea of forgetting about real life while we're here." He frowns, and I have a feeling he has something on his mind, something he'd like to forget about while he's here, but can't bring himself to tell me. Maybe he is thinking of taking his folks up on their offer after all, and like me, is just going to enjoy this week for what it is.

"I like it too. Let's not talk of home, or anything that upsets us. Let's just enjoy the cabin, okay?"

"Okay," he agrees.

I take a bite of trout and moan as the flavor explodes on my tongue. "This is delicious. I thought you didn't know how to cook."

He pounds his chest and I laugh. "I am man. Man knows how to barbecue."

"You're such a goof."

Catching me by surprise, he puts his hand around my head and drops a kiss so tender, so steeped in passion, on my lips, I'm sure my heart is about to explode in my chest. I stare at him as he stares back, his eyes dark, full of passion and...happiness.

I stare at his kissable lips as he talks. "Have you ever thought about sex under the stars?"

My entire body warms as he puts his palm on my cheek and lightly brushes his thumb over my warming flesh. "It's on my bucket list."

"You know I'm all about lists."

"And jars," I add with a chuckle, my body heating all over as it craves his warm touch.

He laughs quietly with me. "We'll get to the jar tomorrow. Tonight, lets concentrate on that list."

He stands and pulls me up with him. Big hands wrap around my body and his hardening cock presses against me as he pulls me to him. I might be addicted to this guy, and that's downright scary.

"Hey," he whispers as he dips his head and lightly brushes his lips over mine. He breathes me in and holds his breath, like he's savoring my scent. My hands go around his back and his muscles ripple everywhere I touch, and I want to touch him without any clothes between us. Although want isn't the right word. It's more like need.

"Hey yourself," I whisper, and slide my hands under his shirt. He quivers, and I run my fingers over his stomach, surfing over the hills and valleys, and reveling in the way his muscles flinch and his body trembles. He reaches over his back, grips his shirt and tugs it over his head.

I moan in sheer appreciation. "That's much better."

"Not really," he says, and I tear my gaze from his naked chest to look at him. He takes my hands. I really love the way his palms swallow mine. It doesn't make me feel small, or vulnerable. It makes me feel safe and secure...cherished. "You're still dressed."

I laugh at that and step back. His fingers fall from mine and his hands dangle idly at his sides. I glance at the house, then out at the lake, and he instantly understands my concerns.

"We can go inside if you like."

I shake my head. "Bucket list."

He takes a small, measured step toward me. "Just know this, no one is going to see you but me. I won't allow that. You're mine, Anna. Everything about you is mine to protect and that includes your body."

My throat tightens to the point of pain as tears prick my eyes. No one has ever said anything so incredibly sweet to me before.

His eyes narrow in on me. "You trust that, right?"

"I trust you," I whisper and it does something to him. He straightens up, his shoulders square as he goes to his full height. A commander. A leader. A protector. An alpha male about to shield what belongs to him, and dammit, I love everything about this.

Without words, I tug on the hem of my T-shirt and peel it over my head. His gaze drops as he blatantly watches. Feeling safe and worshiped as he follows my every movement, I shamelessly—without modesty—unbutton my shorts and shimmy them down my legs. I want this man to do whatever he wants to me tonight and pray he'll finally puts his cock inside me.

"You are beautiful, Anna."

"Thank you." I don't shy away from the comment. Instead, I own it, and reach behind my back to unhook my bra, and my panties follow quickly. His gaze moves over my body, lit only by the stars and moon. He kicks off his shorts, and his hard cock reaches out to me. I step up to him and drop to my knees.

"Anna..." His murmur curls around me as I lean forward and take him to the back of my throat. "It has never been this good for me, and I've not even been inside you yet."

My heart stalls at the honesty in his voice. He's not lying, not waxing poetic crap just to get in my panties, which are now laying on the ground. I lift my head and our eyes lock. "I know I'm going to be your first, but—"

"I wouldn't want any other man but you to be my first, Alek. I have nothing to compare this to, but I also know in my body and heart that nothing else could compare."

His body relaxes, and I might be young, but I'm wise enough to know something potent is going on here, something powerful blossoming between us—something I might not be able to come back from. It's as scary as it is exhilarating, and I guess that's what happens when one lets go of reality to live in fantasy. When we go back home, I realize it's back to the real world, but until then, I'm going all in and praying when I walk away, my heart is in my chest and not in his palm.

I take him back into my mouth, and savor the taste of him. He rocks his hips into me, and his groans curl around me. I love everything about this, but he puts his hands on my shoulders to stop me. I let him lift me, and he walks me to the wharf, stopping at the small boathouse to get a blanket. My heart misses a beat at his thoughtfulness.

He lays the blanket out on the dock and lays flat on his back. I stare at him, not sure what it is he wants me to do, but he grins, and crooks his fingers. He's going to guide me through this.

"Come here, babe. Put your legs around me and sit on my face. I want to taste your sweet pussy."

Oh, God, I love when he says things like that. I straddle him and his hands go to my hips to control my body as I lower myself down on him, and I love how he takes charge of me. I set my knees on the blanket on either side of his head, and his tongue snakes out to lick my pussy and a whimper catches in my throat. It's followed by a chuckle, as I glance around. Sound travels over water and I don't want the neighbors grabbing their binoculars to see what the hell is going on at Alek's place.

I soon forget about the lake, and the neighbors as he pulls me down, holding me securely as he buries his face in my pussy. I involuntarily roll my hips, and rub myself all over him, taking everything he's offering.

"Yes, Alek," I moan, and rock a little harder. He eats at me until I'm burning up, so close to losing it. He lifts me slightly, and a cool lake breeze washes over my wet sex and the hot and cold stimulation shudders through me.

"Go up on your knees." His voice is hoarse and rough, a good sign that he's loving this as much as I am, and that he too is losing control.

I go up on my knees and he slides a thick finger inside me. I cup my breasts, rub my nipples and his groan fills the silence of the night.

"Fuck, I love when you touch yourself," he murmurs, his finger working magic inside me. He inches up, takes my clit into his mouth, and the trifecta—my hands on my breasts, his finger inside me and his mouth on my clit—wrings a powerful orgasm from my body.

"Oh, God, yes!" I scream, as I release all over his face. He laps at me, swirls his tongue all over me, and I move my hips, roll with each powerful wave. The last clench has me bending over, and he pulls his finger from my pussy and holds me up so I don't faceplant.

With strength and ease he slides me down his body until my mouth meets his. Beneath the moon, his wet lips glisten with my juices and he puts one hand around my head and pulls my mouth to his. He kisses me deeply, his tongue tasting every inch of me, as I savor the flavor of myself.

"I love making you come," he whispers into my mouth.

"Seems like our hobbies mesh because I love when you make me come." His soft, playful laugh seeps under my skin and fills me with happiness. When was I ever this happy?

"Do you want my cock inside you?"

"More than anything."

He rolls until I'm beneath him, and I love the weight of his body on mine. "Even if it ruins you?"

I wrap my hands around his head, and bring his mouth to mine. "Please ruin me, Sir."

He briefly closes his eyes. "Fuck girl, *you're* the one ruining *m*e."

He grumbles a little more under his breath, and I'm not sure what he's saying. At the moment, I don't have enough synapses firing to figure it out, not when his cock is between my legs, brushing against my sex.

"Fuck," he blurts out, and I stiffen. What the hell? Why is he upset? Did I do something wrong, or is he having second thoughts? "Oh, sorry." His voice is lower as he softly runs his hands over my hair. "I forgot to grab a condom, they're inside. I just don't want to leave you. Not just because I don't want to stop touching you, but I don't want to leave you out here alone. I promised to protect you, and I never back down on my word."

My insides turn to mush as a little burst of warmth tugs at my trembling heart. Could this rough and rugged man be any sweeter? It completely lowers my inhibitions.

"I'm on the pill," I whisper quietly. He nods in understanding, but I continue with, "I use it to regulate my periods."

He goes silent, and I can almost hear his brain racing, some war going on inside of him. God, was that stupid of me? Am I being young, and reckless, and ridiculous?

"Anna, are you sure?"

"This is my first time, Alek. I think I want to experience it without latex between us."

What are you doing, girl?

No idea.

"I'm clean," he assures me. "I haven't been with anyone in a long while."

"I'm clean too." That brings a smile to his face, because duh, of course I'm clean. I'm a damn virgin.

His warm palm closes over the side of my face, and there's almost a tortured look in his eyes. "I love how much you trust me."

"You won't hurt me," I say, matter of factly, and without thinking.

Every muscle in his body tenses, and he stares at me like a man possessed, like a goddamn caveman ready to go into protective mode. I'm not sure I've ever seen this kind of intensity in him before. My heart jumps in my chest, and my stomach goes tight.

"Anna...is someone hurting you?"

Oh, crap.

"No," I say quickly, anxious to soothe his worries. While I'm deeply touched that he is so worried about me, tonight isn't about my past. "I'm okay. I didn't mean it like that."

"Promise."

"I promise," I say, and move against his body to bring his attention back to our need for one another. "Please...touch me. I need your hands on me."

"Yeah? You need me to touch you...everywhere?" he asks, and even though he's a strong, confident man, I sense a desperate urgency in him. He needs me to want him—needs to hear it.

I take his hand and put it between my legs. "Yes, and you should start here."

He growls as he shifts to his side and slides a finger into me. "I will give you what you need, Anna." He moves a finger in and out of my slickness and I whimper as he finger fucks me. "I can make you feel really good."

"Yes," I moan. "I love that. I love the way you feel inside me." I put my hand over his wrist and move with him as he finds my hot bundle of nerves and strokes. My brain takes a hiatus as pleasure grips me, my world turning upside down and inside out.

He works his finger in me longer, and it's clear he's preparing me for his cock. I resist the urge to scream hallelujah.

"I love the way your body opens for me. So wet and slick." He pulls his finger out to show me. "Look at you, so wet and needy for me." He slides his finger between his lips and a sound catches in my throat as he moans with pleasure. "I love the taste of you."

"Alek," I murmur, complete, coherent sentences a thing of the past.

"Let see how two fingers feel." He slides another one in and I moan at the glorious fullness. "My cock can't wait to be in here. It's all I've thought about since I first set eyes on you. But I would never take you before you were ready."

Tears fill my eyes as my throat squeezes. He cares about me. Wants to make this good for me. I'm not sure any other guy would treat me with such delicate care. I'm sure whoever my folks are trying to set me up with wouldn't take the time to prepare me. My heart wobbles as our eyes meet, and it's possible I'm falling a little deeper in love.

Oh, God, careful, Anna.

"Please put your cock in me, sir."

He shifts and positions himself on top of me, and lines up his big cock at my entrance. I widen my legs and bend my knees. I don't even care if it hurts. I want this more than I've ever wanted anything else in life. Even my freedom, which is absolutely insane.

Eyes full of tender concern meet mine, and my breath stalls in my lungs, as his warmth and gentleness surround me like a soft hug. "This might hurt at first." He curses lightly. "You know that the last thing I want to do is hurt you, right?"

"I do." I take in a deep breath and hold it.

He presses his forehead against mine. "I'm going to need you to breathe, babe."

"Breathing, right," I say and expel the breath I'd been holding.

"I'll breathe with you."

I nod, and we both take deep breaths in and let them out slowly. We repeat this as he moves his hips, his cock breaching my opening. With every intake of breath, he pushes in a bit deeper and a tight ring of pain spreads through my sex, radiating outward from our points of connection.

He goes completely still. "You good, Anna?"

I move my body to encourage him to continue. "Yes," I murmur, and I am good. I'm great, really. He goes deeper and deeper and I breathe with him through the initial pain. Once he's inside, he goes completely still and his smile is tender and filled with sweetness.

"I'm all the way inside you, babe." I kiss him, and wrap my arms around his back. "How does it feel?"

"Full, and amazing."

He rocks his hips, and I'm so wet he easily glides in and out. He continues the smooth, steady motion for a long time, and we breathe as he stretches me. Then something happens in my body, it relaxes around his cock, takes on the shape of him, and the pain changes to pleasure, each gentle thrust taking me to some far-off place I've never been before. I go with it, let my body soar until I'm not sure where my body ends and his begins.

"Alek, that is so good."

"Yeah, that feels so good," he agrees, his entire body tight as I run my fingers over his back, wanting my hands on every inch of him. We rock together and cling to one another, like our lives might depend on it. He grunts against my throat, his body damp and warm against mine as he sends pleasure to every inch of my body. I move beneath him, a little more desperation about me. He must sense it because his rhythm and pace change.

Since I can no longer seem to fill my lungs, I begin to gasp each breath, my body on fire and in need of release. As if knowing exactly what I need, he grinds his pelvis against my clit with each downward thrust. I'm lost. So goddamn lost in this man, in the pleasure he's gifting me, it's going to take a compass for me to find my way out, but at the moment, I don't even care.

"Alek," I murmur and curl into him as a powerful orgasm rips through me. I claw at him, my body quivering around his pistoning cock as I coat him in my hot juices.

"Jesus." His curses echo in the night as I continue to spasm around him, clenching and tightening around his thick girth until his body goes still and he throws his head back and fills me with his seed.

"Ohmigod, I feel you."

He grunts, and drives impossibly deeper, hitting my cervix as he depletes himself, and tears prick my eyes as my heart thuds. Euphoria. That's the only word I can think of to describe what I'm feeling. I never should have waited so long to do this, but it probably would never be this good with any other man.

He cradles my head in his hands and kisses me, his breath hot on my face. It's a soft barely-there kiss, and as our lips linger, the intimacy between us intensifies, which is crazy, considering he just fucked me. While I don't know a hell of a lot, or anything about fucking, I get a sense this was more than just a physical act. Maybe that's just my stupid fantasy brain going into overdrive. I really shouldn't let my imagination get away on me like that. But at the moment, with my stupid heart getting involved, I can't seem to help it.

He slowly inches out of me, and I make a small whimpering sound when he's completely withdrawn from my body. He leans back on his knees, and swipes a finger over my thigh. He lifts his hand. "You bled a little."

Embarrassed, I swallow and I'm about to scurry back, desperate to dash inside to clean up, when his big hand lands on my leg to stop me.

"Hey, I'm a grown-ass man. I'm not afraid of a little blood."

Okay, now that was a reaction I didn't expect. Probably because I'm used to the boys from high school making fun of a girl's period. But Alek is no boy, he's all man. "Don't ever shy away from me, Anna."

"I won't." He wipes the blood on his T-shirt, and a burst of warmth goes through me. God, I could so easily fall for this man. Wait, haven't I done that already? Damn it.

"Let's get you cleaned up."

He stands and helps me to my feet. Before I can take a step, he snatches the blanket, and scoops me up into it. My heart thuds as I wrap my arms around him and hold on. He carries me to the bathroom and closes the door behind us. As he drops to his knees to run water into the tub, I glance into my cosmetic bag. I'd left it in the bathroom earlier after brushing my teeth. I move a few things around and my heart suddenly stops beating, beads of perspiration breaking out on my well used body.

Shit, where the hell are my birth control pills?

ALEK

"Everything okay?" I ask Anna as she takes her last bite of toast and follows it with a big gulp of coffee, like she's stalling, because she doesn't want to answer my question. "Anna?" Christ, I took her virginity last night and I pray to fuck she's not regretting it now.

As my body tightens with worry, she nods and gingerly sets her cup down. "Perfectly fine." Her hand goes to her mouth, and she covers it as she fakes a yawn. Why is she faking a yawn? We talked about honesty and how important it is to me. "Just tired."

Okay, now that I can believe. After her bath last night, I tucked her into her bed, but couldn't bring myself to leave her. Instead, I crawled in beside her and when I grew hard just from snuggling her, and she insisted she wasn't too sore to take me again, I rolled her under me and we made love a second time.

Made love?

I mean we *fucked* and it was pretty goddamn awesome.

"Daddy, I want to go swimming," Chase says.

I glance outside. It's early morning, but it's easy to tell it's going to be a scorcher. "We can do that."

"Is there a town nearby?" Anna pipes in. "A drugstore maybe?"

My gaze goes to hers, and she glances down and stares into her cup. "Do you need something?"

"I just...oh, I have this headache." She crinkles her nose, and goes back to sipping her coffee.

"I have medicine in the bathroom. I'm sure I have something for headaches."

"Oh, okay." She nods and fidgets slightly. "What about a place for souvenirs? Are there any quaint shops nearby?"

What the fuck is going on here? She's acting cagey. "We can go find a souvenir shop later, if you like."

She waves her hand. "Oh no, you don't have to take me. You and Chase should enjoy the morning. I'm sure like most men, you don't like shopping."

I watch her as she picks at her toast, and okay, I get it. She wants a bit of time to herself. I'm not going to keep her here with us if she needs a reprieve. She can take the SUV and head out to find a souvenir shop herself if that's what she wants.

I stand, and grab the keys from the counter. "If you need directions to town, the SUV has a navigation system."

A smile lights up her face as relief moves into her eyes. "Thanks. Would you like me to pick something up for you?"

I sit back down. "No, we're good, and whatever you buy, use my credit card." She looks like she's about to protest, so I hold my hand up. "I insist."

Her smile is soft. "As soon as I get back, I'll dig into the to-do jar."

She glances at the jar above the sink, all the little notes tucked inside. I don't bother to tell her the to-do jar here is for me, and the maintenance that needs to be done. Later this afternoon, I'm going to get started on the repairs to the back deck.

She stands. "I'll get these dishes done and get out of here."

"We can do the dishes." I glance at Chase as he finishes his toast. "Right, little man?"

"I don't want to do the dishes," Chase grumps. "I want to swim."

"We can swim, after the dishes. Also, the neighbors down the road invited us for dinner tonight, remember. You're going to get to play with their son, Nick." They'd only briefly met last night when they popped over with the fish, and while Nick is a couple years older than Chase, they both have a love of Fortnite.

Chase throws his arms up in the air. "Yay, I can't wait to play Fortnite."

There you have it.

Anna brushes crumbs from her hands over her plate, and I take in her loose-fitting sundress. "Are you sure you don't mind doing the dishes?"

"Not at all. Go ahead, have fun."

She nods quickly, dashes to the bathroom and then gives me a little wave as she heads out the door, obviously in a hurry to get to some souvenir shop, which is odd. I haven't seen her text or phone anyone since she's been with me—even back home—so I have no idea who she's buying for. She's clearly had a falling out with her parents, so I doubt they're on her gift list.

Tires crunch as Anna backs out of the driveway, and Chase and I get at the dishes. Once we're done, we head to the lake and spend the next hour or so playing and swimming and laughing. As the morning slips by, I can't fight the unease in my gut. Anna should have been back by now. Maybe I should shoot her off a text, if I can get decent reception.

"Come on, Chase. Time to go in. You can play video games. I'm going to work on the back deck, okay."

"Okay."

We're both waterlogged as we climb from the lake, and my stomach growls as we head into the house. Chase rushes to his room to get changed. I go to my room, strip off, and run a towel over my body. Once dry, I pull on a pair of cargo shorts, not bothering with a T-shirt. It's too damn hot for that. I head out back, the sun shining on me when tires crunching announce Anna's arrival.

I walk around the front of the cottage, and she's worrying her bottom lip as she puts the SUV into park. I step up to her, and she plasters on a smile.

"Did you find what you were looking for?" I ask.

She picks up a bag. "I found a few small things." She rattles the brown paper bag, and it sounds like metal hitting metal. "Some keychains."

"Anything else?"

She once again worries her lip. "No, just these."

I open her door and she slides out. Before she can dash into the cottage, I take her hand in mine. "Is everything okay?" She eyes me, like she wants to say something, but instead goes completely quiet. "Last night—"

"Last night was perfect," she says quickly, and goes up on her toes to kiss me. "You were perfect, Alek."

A wave of relief rolls through me. "You seem a bit distracted today. I thought you might have been having regrets."

"Just a lot on my mind."

"Hey," I murmur. "I thought we were going to forget about real life while we're here."

She nods, and smiles up at me. "You know what, you're right. It's not like I often, or ever, get to just kick back and relax. I can worry about the future when we return."

I put my hand on her back and we walk into the cottage. My guess is she's worried about getting into culinary school. She doesn't strike me as the kind of girl who likes others to call in favors, but this is important to her, so it's important to me too, which is why I'm going to make some inquiries to the school here in Chicago without her knowing it. What she doesn't know can't hurt her, right? In the end if it gets her to where she needs to go, then why not?

Inside the cottage, Chase is sitting on the sofa playing his video game, and Anna drops her bag of souvenirs in her room. She comes back out and I nod to the back door. "I'm repairing the steps." Her gaze rakes over my half naked body and she nods.

"Okay, I'll see what I can find in the jar."

I grin as she steps up to it and pulls out a little piece of white paper. She frowns, and I bite back a laugh. "Um, how does one go about replacing the loose shingles on the roof."

I take the paper from her. "This one is for me." I open the drawer, scribble something on a note, and put it in the jar. "Try again."

She laughs as she pulls out the note I just added. "Ah, this I can do. Lemonade and lunch. I'm on it, sir."

I just shake my head as she goes to the fridge, and as she bends, aiming her sweet ass my way, it's my cue to leave before I get a boner. Back outside, I grab the lumber from the shed, and pull out the table saw. I get to work on measuring and cutting, and before I can nail it down, Anna comes out, a tray in her hand.

"Chase is eating inside. Do you mind if I join you out here?"

"Not at all."

She glances at the three steps, the top one missing, as that's the one I'm replacing first.

"Um, how do I do this without breaking my neck?"

"Here let me take that from you." I reach up, and grab the tray. I set it down, and hold my hand out for her. She takes it and I balance her as she carefully negotiates the stairs. Once she's on the ground with me, I pick up the tray and carry it to the picnic table near the swing set. I take a sip of lemonade, grab half a sandwich, and sit on the swing. She does the same, and we both go quiet as we eat.

"Thanks for making lunch," I say, and think about how to guide the conversation without bringing reality into the afternoon. "This is pretty much the best sandwich I've ever had."

She laughs. "Gourmet grilled cheese. It's all about the gouda."

"Will you be putting this on your menu when you open your own restaurant?"

"I want to do comfort food, but make it upscale, so maybe."

I take another bite of the gooey cheese and moan. "This is so good."

"I'm so glad you like it," she says with a laugh, her demeanor much lighter than it was earlier this morning.

"Are you still set on going to New York for culinary school?"

She kicks at the grass beneath her swing and sets herself into motion. "It's the plan."

"I think you should go to school in Chicago. I'd be your guinea pig, and eat whatever meal you want to try." I arch a brow. "I do have that awesome kitchen back at the house."

"I've always had my heart set on New York, you know. Just to experience other places, but I guess in my heart I realize that might just be a pipe dream."

Fuck, I hate seeing her sad, and I'm being a selfish bastard, wanting to keep her here...for me.

"Is it money holding you back?" I ask blatantly.

"Yeah, and it's a pretty elite school. I'm not sure I can get in without any experience, or references, and the funding might kill me."

"How can you get experience?" I could definitely be a reference for her here, if I call in some favors.

"Working at restaurants, becoming someone's sous chef. My experience is limited to..."

"To what?"

"To cooking at home. I've only had experience in my family's kitchen." She goes quiet for a second. "Staying in Chicago...I guess I should consider it. Cooking for you and gaining experience in your kitchen isn't a hardship."

"Don't settle, Anna. Don't ever settle."

She smiles and bites her sandwich. "I won't and I don't consider Kendall College settling. It's an amazing school." She goes quiet, lost in thought as she kicks her legs out and I enjoy the comfortable quiet between us as we finish eating. Once I'm done, I stand.

"Do you want to help with the deck?"

"I'd love to," she says, eagerness all over her face. "I was never allowed..."

I narrow my gaze, and take her in. "Never allowed to do what?"

"I just...I was sheltered, is all. My parents, I guess they thought I was incompetent or something. But how can you learn without ever trying?"

I can definitely see why she wants to experience more. I think someday I'd like to meet these parents of hers and set them straight. A gorgeous, talented woman like Anna should be flying high, not married off without ever experiencing life. If she were my wife, I'd make sure she had all the experiences she ever wanted. But that's ridiculous thinking. Anna can never be my wife.

Why the hell not?

Oh, because it's not what she wants, dude.

Wait, is it what I want?

"You're right. Come on. Let's teach you how to repair rotting steps."

"Thanks," she says her voice low and soft.

"For what?"

"For bringing me here, for believing in me…for last night."

My cock instantly hardens as memories of last night flood me. "We're just getting started, Anna. We're just getting started."

That's the problem though, we're starting something that will soon come to an end, and I don't like it. Not one little bit.

ANNA

The night air is warm, and a breeze blows in off the lake as we head to Debra and Jack's cottage, just around the bend from Alek's. Their place is shrouded in foliage and trees, much like Alek's, giving them privacy. Chase is running ahead of us on the road, and Alek is carrying the berry dessert I made, a bottle of wine tucked under his arm. I wanted to help but he refused.

"It was so nice of your neighbors to invite us," I say. Out here, I don't have to worry about one of my father's men finding me, and I haven't felt this free in...ever.

Alek glances at me, looking so handsome in his polo shirt, his face freshly shaven. "You know they think we're a couple."

"I know." I crinkle my nose. "Do you think we should straighten them out?"

He laughs. "No. We have sex written all over us, Anna. I'm sure it's easy to tell we've been sleeping together and I'd rather them think we are a couple rather than them thinking I'm messing around with my son's nanny. There's a whole lot wrong with that, and not just because it would get you in trouble with the agency."

I lift my chin an inch. "I don't think there's anything wrong with it at all."

He arches a brow, begging to differ. "I'm in a position of power over you and that makes it a pretty big issue."

"I'm pretty sure I'm the one with the power over you, sir," I say with a grin.

He laughs, and it comes out deep and tortured. "You're not wrong. But I'd prefer it if they thought we were a couple." I frown as I consider that and note the way Alek is eyeing me. "Is that so bad, Anna? Would it be horrible to be my girl?"

Horrible?

Hell no, it would be the most wonderful thing in the world, which is why living in this fantasy is hard, because soon enough, this pretending will have to stop, and my heart might not be strong enough to handle the loss when I have to walk away. I can't forget who my father is, and how he could hold Alek and Chase over my head if I don't do things his way. My stomach clenches so hard, a little sound catches in my throat.

"Are you okay?"

"Yes, just a bit of a cramp."

"Is it your period?"

His question catches me by surprise and I just shake my head in wonderment. It's so strange to me how this man talks so openly about such things. "No, I just had a little twinge, nothing to worry about." I stop before saying I hope—pray— my period is coming.

"Tonight, you should definitely rest." He frowns, like he's upset with himself—blames himself for my distress—and I hate that. What we did last night was amazing, and something I plan to hold close to my heart for the rest of my life, especially on the nights when I move and I'm all alone. My stomach cramps again, but this time it's brought on by the thoughts of leaving Alek and Chase. His arm brushes my shoulder as he moves closer and says, "Maybe we shouldn't have had sex twice last night."

"Yes, we should have," I blurt out and it brings a smile to his face. Although he's right. We probably shouldn't have had sex once, let alone twice last night, especially after I discovered I'd forgotten my birth control pills. I went to town today to try to find a drugstore with the hopes of getting a morning after pill, but I couldn't find a drugstore. I'm sure one night of sex isn't going to get me pregnant. At least I hope not. How awkward is it going to be if I ask him to use a condom, after practically begging him not to use one? I told him I was on the pill, and I don't want him to think I was trying to trick or trap him in any way.

We reach the neighbors' place and walk around to the back to find them barbecuing near the lake. I put on a smile and push all worries to the back of my brain. I want to enjoy tonight, because I'm not sure how many more enjoyable times I'll have with Alek and his neighbors.

"Anna, Alek, I'm so glad you could make it," Debra says and puts her arm around me. She's obviously a hugger. She bends to see Chase. "Nick is inside waiting for you. Run on in and say hello. Dinner will be ready shortly." Chase runs off and Debra takes the dessert from Alek. "This looks amazing, but you didn't have to bring anything."

"We wanted to," I tell her, and as I use the word *we*, Alek smiles at me, and my heart squeezes. I like using the word we. It makes it feel like we're a united couple, and I guess in a sense, in this ruse, we are.

Once Chase is inside, Alek takes my hand in his. While we're trying to give the impression that we're a couple, we don't want to confuse Chase, and it's weird how conflicted I feel about all this. It's not that I want Chase to think I'm going to be his new mommy, do I?

"Anna is an amazing cook." Alek gives my hand a squeeze. "You're going to love it."

"I'm sure I will." Debra gestures to the beautifully decorated table, walks up to it and sets dessert down. "Please sit, what can I get you to drink?"

As she gestures to the bottles of wine and liquor, I'm once again reminded I'm too young to drink. I notice that Debra has a glass of white wine. Alek puts the bottle down that he brought.

"Thanks for the wine, Alek. Anna, I can open yours if you prefer or we can finish the one I opened before we drink the one you brought."

"I'll have what you're having." There's such an openness to Debra that she's easy to be around. It's not like I had many friends growing up, but I'm pretty sure I could easily be friends with her. That brings a knot to my stomach. When I leave here, I'll be leaving all this behind.

Jack closes the barbecue and shakes hands with Alek. "Glad you could make it."

"Thanks for the invite, and the fish last night was amazing. That was very kind of you."

"Our pleasure." Jack smiles, and lifts his glass in salute. "Do you drink scotch?"

Alek nods. "Sounds great." I smile, loving the comradery Alek and I have with these nice people, who are more Alek's age than mine, but that doesn't seem to matter at all.

I sit at the table, and Debra takes a seat across from me. "We thought the place next door was vacant," she says. "You guys haven't been here all summer."

"Life is busy," I say. "But we're here now, enjoying the place before Chase goes back to school."

"We're so glad." She frowns. "We're headed home at the end of the week to get Nick ready for school. He's excited for fourth grade."

"Where is home?" I ask.

"Edison Park."

"Oh, not far from us. We're on the Gold Coast." I smile as I hear Chase shriek from inside the house. "Chase is looking forward to school. I think," I say with a laugh.

"That will definitely free up your time. Are you a stay-at-home mother like me?" she asks, and I note the way Alek's gaze strays my way.

"I'm not his mother." I take a moment to consider what life would be like if Alek and I were a real couple and I had the privilege of raising his son. The idea doesn't sit well with me, mainly because I like it too much, and a future with Alek is out of the question. I can't bring him and his son into my world, and by rights I shouldn't even be here with him. But I am and it's too late to turn back now, which means I need to forget about real life and just enjoy as much of this as I can.

"Oh, sorry. I didn't mean to pry. I just assumed he was your son."

"Don't be sorry." I take a sip of wine. "Alek and I haven't been together that long, and even though Chase isn't my biological son, I do love the boy." I don't turn, but can feel Alek's eyes on me. The heat in his stare warms my blood and okay, it's true, I might love Chase's father too.

Oh boy.

Changing the subject, I say, "I assumed you were an interior decorator. This table, your place, everything looks amazing."

"That's so nice of you to say. I dabble in it a bit. Maybe someday when Nick is older, I'll take some courses."

She glances at my ring finger. "You and Alek aren't married?"

"Not yet, no," Alek pipes in, his words and firm voice taking me by surprise.

"Oh, so there's a wedding in the future. How exciting!" Debra leans in a little. "Tell me all about it."

"Debra, let her breathe, they just got here." Jack grins at me. "Sorry about the interrogation. Most of the people on the lake are much older than us, and Debra is desperate for conversation with someone her age."

I laugh at that. "I don't mind the questions at all. How long have you two been married?" I ask.

"Eight years." She winks at me. "I was a child bride." I laugh. If Dad makes me marry, I'll be the child bride. "We were married at the Greenhouse Loft. Jack is an architect, and his firm had a hand in designing it."

"You're an architect? That's amazing." I glance at Alek, who is keeping a close eye on me. Not to control me but to make sure I'm comfortable, and I sort of love that. "Alek is a lawyer. Best in Chicago."

He laughs. "I wouldn't go so far as to say that. Anna is a chef. Best in Chicago, and I can say that because she made me the best grilled cheese sandwich today."

Everyone laughs, and heat travels into my cheeks at the compliment. "Well, I wouldn't go so far as to agree to that. I haven't been to culinary school yet."

"I didn't know I was going to be cooking for a chef," Jack says with a laugh as he lifts the barbecue lid. "Talk about pressure."

"Don't be silly. I'm sure it's delicious."

Debra laughs. "Have you decided on your venue yet?"

"No, but I'd like something near a lake. I'm not interested in a big traditional church wedding." That's what my father expects, but that's from his era, not mine, and honestly, I'm not the fairy tale girl who dreams of her wedding.

"That sounds lovely," she says, and points to the lake. "This would be a perfect spot."

"You're right." I stare out over the lake and take in their boat. I breathe in the fresh air and my entire body relaxes as I let it out and for the first time in my life, I visualize my wedding. Only problem is the groom waiting for me is none other than Alek.

"Dinner is ready," Jack announces.

Debra stands and smooths her hand down her dress. "I'll get the boys."

"What can I do to help?"

"There are some salads in the fridge. Would you mind grabbing them?"

I follow her inside, and the sound of laughter fills the house and my soul. I love the sound of the boys playing. I don't remember too much laughing in my house growing up. I open the fridge and take out a vegetable salad and potato salad.

The boy rush out the door ahead of me, followed by Debra, and my heart is so full as I carry the food to the table. We all sit, and Jack places platters filled with grilled steak and lobster down.

"This is lovely."

"Dig in," Jack says with a big smile. Alek helps Chase fill his plate and I smile at the love between the two.

A hand closes over mine and Debra says quietly, "It's so easy to see how much you all love each other."

My heart wobbles. Is it possible that my two guys feel the same way about me as I feel about them? Do I dare hope? Wait, no, I can't hope. My father would never allow me to make my own choices where love and relationships are concerned. It's best they don't feel for me what I feel for them, otherwise it could be disastrous, and I can't—won't—let either of them get caught in the middle of my problems.

We all fall into easy conversation, and I'm sipping my third glass of wine, which is going straight to my head. I start chuckling a lot, my inhibitions weakening, and once the dessert has been eaten, Alek reaches for my hand.

"I think we should get you to bed." He grins at Debra. "She's a lightweight."

Debra nods and looks at the wine bottle. "That one has put me to bed early a time or two," she teases in understanding.

We all stand, and Chase complains about leaving, but Debra assures him he can come back and even when we're all back home, the boys can be friends. Chase runs ahead, and with his arm around me, Alek leads me to the road, and he's smiling down at me when I lift my gaze to his.

"Are you feeling okay?"

"I'm feeling great." I hiccup, and laugh as I throw my hand over my mouth.

"Yeah, I can tell. Let's get you to bed."

"I like that idea," I say, although something is niggling in the back of my brain, something I can't quite grasp on to. "Alek."

"Yeah."

"Why did you want to become a lawyer?"

He goes quiet for a moment, and I worry I touched on a soft spot. "I lost a friend once. He got shot. It was a senseless death."

"How did he get shot?"

"He got caught in the middle of a turf war."

I gasp. "I think I remember reading about that." I also remember thinking my father's men might have had something to do with it. "I'm so sorry."

"I just want to right the wrongs, you know."

"I know. I really like that about you."

We reach the cottage, and Alek ushers Chase to bed, and then proceeds to take me to my room, and undress me. His gaze is ravenous as he tucks me in, and he's about to leave but I reach for him.

"I need you."

His muscles tense. "You've been drinking, Anna. I won't take advantage of that."

"No, you shouldn't, and I love that you're a gentleman. But I think you should take advantage of me, sir."

His growls rush over my skin and stroke my warm sex. "Are you sure?"

I push the blankets off and spread my legs. His gaze drops to my hand as I reach between my legs and stroke myself.

"Fuck, Anna."

"Yes, please..."

He locks the door, rips his polo off and kicks away his shorts. It only takes him seconds to get naked and climb over my body. Big fingers brush my hair from my face.

My gaze moves over his face. "I liked pretending we were a couple tonight."

"Me too."

I run my hands through his hair and bring his mouth to mine for a fiery kiss. He moans into my mouth, as he slips a hand between our bodies to prepare me for his cock. One thick finger easily slides in and out. I'm so wet and ready it's insane.

"I love how wet you get for me." He pulls his hand out and in a smooth quick thrust, he's inside me and I'm clawing at his back as I try to get air. He rocks his hips and grunts as he fucks me, and I love every second of it.

"More," I cry out shamelessly, as once again something niggles in the back of my brain, but I'm too aroused to bring it to the forefront. I lift my head, lightly bite his shoulder as he fills me, and I cling to him as a powerful orgasm rocks through me.

"Yes," he growls as I squeeze around him, and a second later, he splashes inside me, his heat filling my core and traveling onward and outward. "So good, Anna."

"So good," I agree. He collapses over me, his cock still inside my body, and I close my eyes, sleep pulling at me. But the next thing I know, my eyes are wide open and I'm staring at a face as equally alarmed as mine.

"You heard it too?" I ask.

ALEK

"Daddy, I don't want to go to school."

"But you want to see who's in your class, don't you?"

"I can't leave Gus."

Gus, of course, is his new turtle and he had to name him after the turtle from the museum. Right after we left the cottage last night, we went straight to the pet store to pick him up. I decided to wait on the pup until we get turtle life figured out. It was late when we hit the pet store, so we got the bare essentials and I told Chase we could go back out after school and get him some toys.

"Gus will be here when you get back. Now let's hurry." I glance up and find Anna packing a sandwich into his new lunch box. She has a smile on her face, but there's something different about her. Ever since she had too much wine, and we ended up making love, she's been back to being skittish. Always looking over her shoulder. We both heard a noise outside my cottage that night, and I went to look, but no one was there. I assured her it was probably an animal trying to get into the trash, but she didn't seem convinced. She'd also asked me to go back to using a condom, which was bizarre. Did she need the measure of separation between us for some reason? Did she only want to try skin on skin once, or rather three times, and that was enough? I don't know. There's a lot of things about Anna I don't know.

A part of me wants to do a background check on her, or ask my father to do one, but I don't want the inquisition if I do. Maybe I'm not doing one myself, because well…maybe I just like the things the way they are and I don't want to rock the boat.

Just then my phone rings and it's my father. I slide my finger across the screen. "Hi Dad."

"Son, how are you? Is Chase still there?"

"He's right here." I hand the phone to Chase and he smiles. Dad's voice is so loud, I can hear both sides of the conversation. My heart tightens as Chase's grandfather wishes him a great first day in first grade. My folks really do love their only grandson. Some of my anger at them dissolves. The truth is that they really do want what's best for Chase and me. Maybe Anna is right, and I'll like the woman they want me to marry. Maybe I should give it a chance. Anna finishes packing the lunch, puts it in Chase's backpack, and reaches for the to-do list jar.

Or maybe I should tell them to go to hell and ask Anna if she's interested in the role. But that would be a mistake. She has a life to live yet, and I can't keep her from that.

Fuck me.

"Bye Grandpa," Chase says and hands the phone back to me. "Come on, Daddy, I don't want to be late."

I shake my head at Anna as Chase gives me whiplash. I snatch his backpack off the counter. "I'll see you around six."

"I'll have dinner waiting."

Christ, I love the idea of her being here for me, far too much. I linger for a second. "Maybe tonight, we could have a quiet night. Sit out by the pool and talk."

"I'd like that," she says, and I glance over my shoulder to make sure Chase isn't watching. I turn back and give her a fast kiss on the lips, and it's hell to pull away.

"What was that for?" she asks, her lids half closed, her mouth still parted.

"Something to think about while I'm gone."

She chuckles and holds the jar up. "I'll have lots to occupy me when you're gone."

"Don't work too hard." I lightly touch her hand.

"Chicken caesar salad okay for dinner?"

"Sounds perfect. Just use the credit card I gave you for anything you need to buy, and the SUV is in the garage if you need to go out."

"I have everything I need here. I don't have to go anywhere."

"Call me if you need anything."

"Daddy, come on."

I back away quickly. "See you tonight, Anna."

"Yeah, you will, sir," she responds, a promising grin on her face, and my stupid dick thickens.

I adjust my pants, and she laughs. "You're going to pay for that."

"Can't wait."

I grumble as I head outside, and walk Chase down the road to the bus stop. I meet up with Theresa and Sophie.

"Hey Theresa," I say and I'm about to say hello to Sophie, but Chase is excitedly telling her about Nick, and the video games they played and of course, his new turtle. "Where's Sophie's new nanny?" Theresa averts her gaze, and it sends warning bells to the back of my brain. "Is everything okay?"

She gives a dismissive wave of her hand. "Everything is fine, we just haven't found anyone suitable for Sophie yet. It's not easy to find a nanny who's worked with special needs children before."

I nod, because I really have no experience with that, and have to take her word on it.

She finally meets my gaze again. "How are things working out with you and Anna?"

Now it's my turn to look away. "Good, Chase really loves her."

"And you..." she asks. I turn to her, unease crawling down my spine at her intrusive question.

"She's working out just fine, Theresa." My words are a bit hard, letting her know this is a conversation I'm not interested in having.

The bus comes, and I'm relieved. Once Chase is onboard, I turn and walk quickly to my car before Theresa can ask any more prying questions. Like my folks, I get she'd like to see me with someone, but she was the one who straight up and told me Anna was too young. Maybe she was trying to play some game with me. Tell me what I can't have so I'll want it more, but why would she care if I'm falling for Anna or not?

Fuck, I'm falling for Anna.

Falling?

Okay, maybe I've fallen already. Hard. Fast. Stupidly.

Once the bus is gone, I back out of the driveway, and as I do, I notice a car on the other side of the road, a man inside. I slow down as an uneasy feeling mushrooms inside me. My mind goes back to Anna, and how I'm worried someone is hurting her. Is it possible that someone was outside my cottage that night?

I circle back around, about to park behind the dark sedan, but it starts up and drives away. I sit there for a moment, and pull my phone from my pocket. Should I message Anna, tell her to be careful? I don't want to frighten her if it was nothing. For all I know that guy could be my tail, but I've never had one stand out so blatantly before. I shoot her off a text.

Me: Hey, just checking in.

Anna: You've been gone a whole 5 minutes.

Me: If you go out let me know, okay?

Anna: Why?

Me: I'm just an overbearing boss who likes to micromanage.

It's a lie, but what am I supposed to say?

Anna: I will. Have a great day at work. I drew the 'dust' card from the jar, so I'd better get at it before my boss gets back. He's kind of a hard ass.

I laugh at that, a bit of the tension easing from my bones. If she plans to stay in, doors locked, I have nothing to worry about, right?

Me: Chase will be home around two.

Anna: I'll be here for him.

I smile and want to tell her she's the best, but I don't. Instead, I toss my phone onto my seat and head to work. I spend the better part of the day going over paperwork, and when the clock hits four, I snatch my jacket off the back of the chair and make a quick departure. I'm calling in a favor and I don't want to be late.

In my car, I hurry across town, headed to Kendall College, Chicago's number one culinary management college. I park, climb out of the car, checking the time as students walk the campus. I go inside and head to the dean's office. Dean Blackmore and I have a common friend, who set this meeting up for me. I hate owing anyone anything, but this is important to Anna, which makes it important to me.

I knock and Dean Blackmore invites me in. Warm scents of leather and old books fill my senses when I step inside and Dean Blackmore stands.

"Alek, so nice to meet you. Jared has such nice things to say about you."

"Thanks for seeing me on such short notice. I appreciate your time."

"Any friend of Jared's is a friend of mine. Although no introduction is needed. Your name precedes you, of course."

I stiffen. Christ, does he know who my father is? "You've heard of me?"

"I've heard of your charitable work, yes. It's an honor to be in the company of such a caring and generous man." I usually like to keep my philanthropy work to help wayward teens a secret but somehow it always leaks out. He waves his hand. "Please, have a seat."

I walk across the room and drop down into a comfy leather chair across from his desk and the Dean sits back down in his chair while smoothing a hand down over his tie.

"What can I help you with?"

"I'm interested in learning about your winter program."

"Ah, yes, I see. Tired of practicing law? Looking to change professions, perhaps?" he asks with a cheeky grin.

I laugh. "No, it's for my son's nanny. She's interested and I'm just helping her out, checking on enrollment and financial costs."

"Has she applied?"

"No, not yet. I believe she's waiting until her finances have improved, but I'm here to help her with that."

"She must be a very good nanny to your son."

He's not being an asshole when he says that. In fact, he seems very sincere. "She is."

"It's very nice of you to help out like this."

He pulls an application from his desk drawer as well as a booklet on all the school has to offer. "Spots are limited, and we're pretty full."

I sink into my chair, my heart falling. Dammit, I was really hoping this would work out, for her, and well, okay, I'm man enough to admit that it's selfishly for me, too. I push back into my chair, ready to offer funding for a new wing, when he slides the application across the desk.

"For you, however. I am sure we can make an exception."

I sit up a bit straighter. "Seriously?"

"Of course, Alek."

I glance over the application. "I don't know how to thank you."

"Have her fill this application out and get it back to me ASAP. The deadline to apply has come and gone, so I will have to get it into the system right away."

"She'll have them filled out tonight." I put the papers into a manila folder, and slide it into my briefcase. "As for financing, I'd like to pay her tuition in full. Today. I'd also like to make a donation to the school."

That brings a huge smile to his face. "How kind of you, sir."

I chuckle when he calls me sir. It doesn't quite have the same effect as when Anna calls me that. "My pleasure, Mr. Blackmore."

He stands. "Please call me Daniel."

"Daniel it is."

"Let me walk you down to finance where you can make all the arrangements."

Thirty minutes later, I'm negotiating traffic, anxious to tell Anna about Kendall College, and praying she's not upset that I overstepped. I realize she had her heart set on New York, but this just makes so much more sense for her. She can live with me, and won't have to worry about rent, and Chase doesn't lose a nanny.

I don't lose the woman I've fallen for.

I park in the driveway and hurry inside the house to find Anna and Chase sitting at the table, going over the drawing Chase did at school. My heart leaps into my throat at the sight. I want this. All of this. With Anna. As if feeling my eyes on her, her head lifts, and for a second I think I spot worry in her eyes.

"Everything okay?"

She smiles. "Everything is fine. You're home earlier than I thought. I don't have dinner prepared. I spent the day doing chores, then Chase came home, and we've been having snacks and chatting about his teacher and classmates, and his colorings."

"You've had a busy day in the house, then?"

"Very busy."

"You didn't go out?" My mind rewinds to the strange vehicle parked near my place.

"Uh, no."

For a second I get the sense she's not telling me the truth, but why would she lie about such a thing?

"Don't worry about dinner. We can order in. Right now, I need to talk to you. Chase, go get your sneakers on. When I'm done talking to Anna, I'll take you back to the pet store."

"Yay!" He jumps from the table and darts into the other room.

"Is everything okay?" she asks tentatively.

I dig the brochure and application form from my bag. "I don't want you to be mad."

"That's not a great way to start a conversation, Alek."

"It's just…you seemed like you were warming to the idea of going to culinary school here, and I had a friend who knew the dean—"

Her hand closes over mine. "What did you do?"

"I talked to the dean today. He has a spot for you in the winter program, if you want it."

She stares at the application so long, everything inside me screams I might have messed up. She's a girl to do things on her own, and she's upset with this.

"Anna, I just want to help."

"You did this…for me?"

Her head lifts, and her eyes are filled with tears. "Hey, come on. Don't be mad."

"I'm not. I just can't believe you would do this for me. It's so sweet."

I relax. "You're not mad?"

"How could I be mad at you, Alek? I just…I don't think I have enough saved for the winter program."

I take her hands in mine. "It's covered."

She gives a hard shake of her head. "No, I can't take your money."

"You're not taking it. You're working for it. Around here, taking care of Chase."

"Alek…"

"Please, Anna. Just say yes."

"Why would you do this for me?"

I take in her big blue eyes, and I'm about to tell her it's because I love her and want to give her the world, when Chase yells out for me to hurry up.

"Can we talk about this tonight?"

She nods, and I lean in and kiss her mouth. "Fill these forms out right away. Use my office computer and scanner to send them back to the address on the top."

"Okay."

She sits there staring at the papers, and as much as I hate to leave, I realize she needs a moment to process and sort this all out. I did sort of just spring it on her. Since Chase's booster seat is still in the SUV, I pop the garage and usher him in. He gets in the back seat, and buckles himself in, talking a mile a minute about his turtle and the toys it needs. I laugh as I climb into the front seat, but the second I do—or at least try—I realize the seat is not where I left it. If Anna didn't go anywhere today, why has the seat been moved to her position?

19

ANNA

I can't seem to tamp down the uneasy feeling inside me as I stand and put the dishes in the sink. Before Alek left to go to the store with Chase, he asked if we could talk tonight, but ever since he returned, he's been quiet, almost angry. Did I do something to upset him? Did I not react the way he wanted after he told me about culinary school? Seriously, it's the sweetest thing anyone has ever done for me, and I can't express my gratitude enough, which was why tonight I planned to show him how much I appreciate what he's doing for me.

"Come on, Chase," Alek calls out to Chase as he plays airplane with his fork. "Bath and bedtime."

Alek pushes from his seat, and walks to the archway separating the kitchen from the living room. He stands there waiting, and Chase jumps up and runs off. As his little feet pound on the stairs, I meet Alek's dark gaze.

"We need to talk, Anna."

"Okay," I say, my stomach tightening. I'm not sure why he's standing there with his brow furrowed, or why he seems so upset, but tonight, I plan to tell him how I feel about him, about his son, and how much I want both of them. It's not wise. My father won't like this one little bit, but if I'm careful, really, really careful, maybe I can have the career and the family I want—the one I chose for myself. I just pray Alek wants the same thing, although I'm beginning to have doubts. His muscles are tight, his jaw clenched, like he's about to deliver bad news and isn't sure how.

Then again, if he wanted me gone, would he have gone to see the dean, and paid my tuition in full? Maybe he's just worried in the end I'll flee. That's what Chase's mother did, right? But I'd never do that to him or Chase and tonight I plan to ease all his worries.

He stands there a second longer. "Did you get your papers sent off to the dean?"

"I have them all filled out and will scan and send them after I'm done the dishes."

"Okay, good." He scrubs his hand over his chin. "Leave the dishes. We can do them later. I'd rather you get the papers sent off right away."

"It's okay. I'll be done with the dishes before you finish with Chase's bath. I can get it all done."

He looks like he's about to say more, but instead closes his mouth and nods. I stare at his back as he turns, and I go back to finishing the dishes, anxious to get the papers off to the dean. I wash and dry the dishes quickly and dart back into Alek's home office. I take a seat in his big, comfy chair and go about scanning my paperwork. Upstairs is quiet, except for Chase playing in the tub, and I take a deep breath, and let it out slowly, totally convinced my life is on the right track.

As soon as I hit send, and lean back in Alek's chair, a noise out back startles me. I spin in the chair, and stare out at the pool, but the sun has set, making it hard to see. I wait for the floodlights to come on, but they never do. I relax a bit, and work to convince myself it was nothing but an animal. Alek assured me that it was likely a raccoon the night we heard a noise at the cottage.

I stand, and stretch, and swallow against a dry throat. Since Alek is still busy with Chase, I head to the kitchen for a drink, and my heart jumps into my throat when I see a man staring at me through the kitchen window. I'm about to run and lock the patio door, but he gets there first, and pushes it open. I try to run but he grabs me, spins me around and puts a hand over my mouth before I can scream at the top of my lungs.

"Not one word." The man's voice is deep, serious...threatening. "I'm going to take my hand off your mouth, but if you make one sound..." He points upward. "You won't like what will happen."

Ohmigod.

I nod, because what else can I do. I'm not about to put Alek and Chase in danger. He removes his hand and I spin around and look up at him with questioning eyes. What does he want from me? I look closer, and that's when I realize it's Bruno, at least I think that's his name, and he's one of my dad's men.

"You're going home."

I want to protest. I want to tell him no. But how can I? I know he won't hurt me. At least I don't think he will, but the other two people in the house... I can't say what he'll do to them.

Tears prick my eyes, and I dig my nails into my palm. This is all my fault. I never should have agreed to be Chase's nanny and Alek's lover. Nothing good would come from it, and I knew that going in. I knew my father would eventually hunt me down and find me if I stayed in Chicago. I just didn't have enough money or the means to leave the state, and now, I've brought nothing but trouble to the family I love.

"How did you find me?" I ask quietly.

"It doesn't matter. All that matters is you're going back home, where you belong."

I want to scream at him, tell him I am where I belong, but I clamp my mouth shut. He won't appreciate an outburst, and it could mean trouble for Alek and Chase.

"I need to grab my stuff."

"You don't need anything."

My heart crashes as my brain races. If I just go missing, my stuff still here, Alek will likely call the police, and that won't be good for anyone. No, it's better if I take my stuff, have him think I left him on purpose. It's hateful and hurtful, but at least that way he won't come looking for me, and find more than he'd bargained for.

"I can't lose my mother's necklace," I tell him, even though I don't have it, but I need this bluff if I'm going to get my belongings. "She'll never forgive me." He opens his mouth, his eyes darker, and I know he's about to protest so I say, "She'll never forgive you."

He curses under his breath. "If this is some sort of trick."

"It's not. I just want to get my things."

"One word. One wrong move, and anything that goes down will be your fault. Got it."

"Got it." I head toward the archway, and he stays on my heels. "You wait here, you'll make too much noise on the stairs. I can get up and down quickly and quietly."

"Move it."

I grab the rail, and knowing which steps squeak, I work around them and head upstairs. Alek's voice reaches my ear, but he's not in the bathroom or Chase's room. He's in his bedroom and he's on his phone. My pulse is beating so hard in my ears it's difficult to hear, but from the sound of his voice, he's not happy.

"I don't think that's necessary," he says to the person on the other end. I press myself against the wall and tiptoe to my room. I quietly gather my belongings and continue to listen to the one-sided conversation.

"A party planner isn't necessary. I just want something simple, Mom. Why do you have to make everything into a big deal?"

My heart stalls in my chest. Is he talking to his mother about a wedding? Has he succumbed to their demands and agreed to take a wife of their choosing?

"Fine, fine. We can do it your way, but I'm not happy about this. You know I hate springing things on Chase. Not everything has to be a surprise, you know."

Is he talking about a wife, and not wanting to spring her on Chase?

"I don't care what kind of flowers. Wait, do we even need flowers? Your backyard is full of foliage as it is." A long moment of silence, and then, "Just do it your way. I don't really care, and no I'm not going to put up a fuss, as you like to call it. For the record, I'm a grown-ass man, I don't fuss. I just want what's right for my son and me."

The more I listen the more I'm convinced he's on the phone with his mother planning his wedding. My throat hurts as I swallow, aches really. Was the tuition and enrollment into culinary school the consolation prize or something? His way of telling me what's between us is over, and that was my parting gift? My God, I think it was. A stupid garbled sound crawls out of my throat and I clamp my hand over my mouth.

"Hang on, I thought I heard something." I go perfectly still and stop breathing. "Anna, is that you?" I close my eyes, and pray Bruno isn't going to come rushing up the stairs guns blazing. Under his breath, Alek mutters, "I'm getting as paranoid as Anna." Is that what he thinks, I'm paranoid? Why wouldn't he? Most times I act like a skittish kitten, with good reason.

He goes back to talking to his mother, and my heart is somewhere in the pit of my stomach as I quietly tiptoe down the stairs. Bruno captures my arm and I yank it back. He might be able to bring me back home, but he doesn't get to touch me. No, the only man allowed to touch me is Alek—and he's preparing for his arranged wedding. Could this be any more messed up?

We head outside, and the night air falls over us, a sense of loss, sorrow and loneliness gripping my soul as I close the door on Alek and Chase. It's hard to do it, but it's going to be even harder to close the door in my mind to all the amazing memories we've made. I hate the thoughts of him thinking I'd run out under the cover of darkness, but I guess, after hearing his conversation, I probably made things easier for him. He no doubt wanted to talk tonight about me leaving, so he could move a new wife in. I have no idea why he suddenly changed his mind about an arranged marriage. He seemed so dead set against it.

A half laugh, half groan rumbles in my throat and Bruno gives me a warning glance. I snarl at him as I realize I'm the reason Alek changed his mind. I straight up told him he might like the girl his parents chose.

Well done, Anna. Well done.

All I can say is I hope the same is true for me, and I like whoever my parents plan to marry me off to. No way on the face of this earth will I be able to escape again. But, if I do marry, maybe I can convince my husband into letting me go to culinary school. Or maybe I can secretly take classes.

I climb into the back of the black sedan without incident, and he quietly closes the door. As I buckle up, he slips into the driver's seat and drives me back to my home. As we approach, the big gates open, gates similar to the ones securing Alek's parents' family home. The gates close behind us, and Bruno talks to someone on his phone. A second later, the front door opens, and my mother and father come rushing out.

I feel a measure of guilt for letting them worry about me, but it's quickly replaced by anger. They want to marry me off to some unknown man, for God's sake.

I step up to them, and my mother throws her arms around me. "Darling, I've missed you."

I inch back, and there isn't worry in her eyes. No worry at all. She's happy, sure, but there's a sparkle there, like she's won some sort of war between us. My shoulders sag, the fight draining from my body. I can't keep doing this. I can't keep running. Maybe my life with this guy won't be so bad. Mom seems happy with Dad, and theirs was an arranged marriage. It's not like Alek wants me, or I would be fighting to stay with him.

"Come inside," my father says, his voice stern.

We head into the massive foyer, and one of the servants serves me a glass of water on a gold tray. My parents lead me to the plush sofa, and I sit. "I didn't mean to worry you," I say.

"You're here now and that's all that matters."

Actually, I know it's not all that matters. All that matters is that I do what they want, and at this point in my life, what other choice do I have?

"How long have you known where I was?"

"Long enough."

I lift my chin an inch. "I want to go to culinary school."

"That will be up to your husband."

I fight back angry tears. I'm angry because I have no way out of this marriage. "This guy...he's okay with an arranged marriage?"

"Yes," my father says.

"He won't mind that I'm not a virgin." Okay, maybe I do have a little bit of fight left in me.

My father snarls, and my mother puts her hand on his lap to soothe him. "You've given yourself to someone else?" he asks.

"Yes."

"Who?" he barks.

"It doesn't matter."

"Was it least an act of love?" my mother asks, and the question takes me by surprise. As does the hope in her eyes.

"Yes."

They both relax on the sofa, and after that crazy adrenaline rush back at Alek's, my body nearly collapses. I yawn, completely exhausted. "Can I go to bed now?"

My mother folds her hands on her lap. "Of course."

"The wedding will be in a couple weeks," Dad declares as I stand.

"Can't wait."

"I'm sure you'll have a wonderful marriage. He's a nice young man."

"Sure," I mutter. He might very well be a nice young man, but he's not Alek, which means he's not the man for me. But I guess I was never the woman for Alek either, so there you have it.

20

ALEK

I hate everything about today. I hate that I'm standing in a church I don't attend, in a goddamn tux I don't want to be in, men at my side that I barely know and a woman I've never met about to be my wife.

Beside me, Chase moves restlessly. I assured him numerous times that he'd like his new mother, but I have no idea if he will or not. Christ, didn't I promise him I would never spring a mother on him? That he didn't have to worry about such things? I'm a man of my word and I've failed my son. I can never forgive myself for that. I had insisted on meeting the woman before this ridiculous ceremony, for Chase's sake, to keep my word to him, but apparently, she flat out refused. Clearly this woman—the only thing I know is her name is Arianna—wants this every bit as much as I do, which is zero percent.

I fidget and catch my mother's eyes. She's smiling, so happy I finally agreed to this. Maybe she's right, maybe she is a better judge of character than me and I should trust her on that. Clearly Anna and I weren't meant to be. After my phone call with my mother that dreadful night, when she was insistent that we have a big backyard birthday party for Chase—which I totally didn't want, but I have learned to choose my battles wisely—I left the room in search of Anna, only to find her and all her belongings gone.

My stomach tightens and I shake my head. What the fuck was I thinking? Falling in love with some young girl who was Chase's nanny. Like my ex, she was just looking to take from me. The second I enrolled her in culinary school and paid for it, she was gone. I guess she got what she needed and had no other reason to stick around. By rights I should have canceled the payment, but I couldn't bring myself to do it. She might have gutted me, ripped me wide open and left me bleeding, but goddammit, I still want to see her succeed in life.

I never did find out why she used the SUV that day, or where she'd gone. I can only guess that it had something to do with her leaving Chase and me. There are still so many questions that haven't been answered, but I guess it doesn't matter now. I'm about to marry another woman and it's time to put Anna out of my mind.

The music changes to the wedding march and my entire body goes stiff. Everyone in the room stands and turns to see the bride walking up the aisle. She has a veil on, which hides her face, and she's watching her feet as she walks. She's either worried she's going to fall, or can't bring herself to face me and while I don't even want to look at her, I find myself staring...find myself recognizing the soft sway of her hips, the familiar curves of her body. My heart misses one beat, and then another.

My God...is it? It can't be? Right?

I suck in air, and hope to get my heart beating regularly again, when the woman and her father stop in front of me. Her head lifts to her father, and he lifts her veil, flipping it over her head. The second she turns to me, the world around me tilts on its axis and I falter backward, right into the minister.

"Anna," Chase yells out and my mother gathers him into her arms.

"What the fuck," I whisper, and a collective gasp goes around the room. Okay, I'm in a church, maybe I shouldn't be swearing, but seriously, what the fuck is going on right now?

"Alek," she whispers, her body shaking.

"Anna, what are you doing here?"

She frowns and her brows pull together. Her gaze goes from me, to her father, then her mother, before it returns back to me.

"Why?" she asks.

"Why?" I blurt out.

She begins to back up, and her father captures her arm in a tight hold. It brings out the protector in me and before I even realize what I'm doing, I rush to her rescue. I take her from her father as his men all stiffen, their hands inches from their weapons. I glance at my side of the church, and they're all poised as well, ready for battle. I blink my eyes hard, and pray this is some kind of crazy dream, or rather nightmare.

"Anna, why?"

"What are you talking about?"

I scan the crowd and when my gaze lands on Theresa as she sinks a little deeper into her seat and turns from me. Jesus Christ, how many people were in on this?

I shake my head, incredulous. "You've been manipulating me this whole time."

"I have no idea what you're talking about." Her father reaches for her, but I glare at him so hard he backs away.

I take her arm. "Come with me."

The crowd goes deadly silent as I pull her to me and lead her to a private room in the back. I close the door and stare at her. "Anna—wait, it's Arianna, right?"

"It's Arianna, but I shortened it to Anna."

"And Miller."

Heat moves into her cheeks. "I shortened that to, because—"

"Because you didn't want me to know who you were. You were trying to trick me, manipulate me into falling for you. How did I not see through you?"

"Why would I do that?" she asks, her voice bordering on hysteria.

"To bring our families together, that's why. You planted yourself at Theresa's and then you all conspired, and faked her firing you..." I run my hand through my hair, messing it up. "Wait, fuck. That's why Emma left in such a hurry. Your father's men must have gotten to her and paid her off." I pace the small room as she stands there before me trembling, and a part of me wants to bring her into my arms and hug her, tell her everything is going to be all right, but how can I do that. She knows honesty is important to me, and then she pulled off the scam of the century.

"How did I ever fall for this?"

"Alek—"

I cut her off, and say, "I guess love really is blind." Tears pour down her face, and I put a shield up around my heart. "Why did you lie to me about not going out in the SUV?"

Her head jerks up. "What?"

"The day you left. You said you never left the house. Where did you go, and why didn't you want me to know?"

She opens her mouth, and I try not to react to the pain on her face. I can't believe how many people were in on this, conspiring to get me to fall for her, to bring the families together. My family told me it was about Chase needing a female influence, but I'm smart enough to know about the feud between the Sicilians and the Russians, and how a marriage can bring families together. Everyone has been lying to me and I'm nothing but the fool of the century.

"Where did you go?" I don't know why it's so important to me, I only know that it is.

"I went...to the drugstore."

I shake my head, barely able to compute as rage burns through my blood. "The drugstore?"

"I...I thought I might be pregnant."

I stumble backward, and fall into a chair. My throat dries as I imagine her with my child—which I'd done numerous times, just never under these circumstances. But wait, is that part of the manipulation too. Tell me she's on the pill, and then trap me with a baby. I guess if they couldn't get me to that altar, they were going to drop that bombshell on me.

"Are you pregnant?"

"No, thank God."

"I thought you were on the pill," I say, my words dripping with accusations.

"I am...I was..."

"Which is it?"

"I forgot them when we went to the cottage, and then we had sex without a condom. More than once."

I snort, happy she's not with my child...I think. "How convenient that you'd forgotten them."

Her shoulders stiffen and she transforms before my eyes. The blue in her eyes turns stormy, and her body tightens, anger radiating from her every pore. There's a dangerous fierceness about her when she asks. "Are you accusing me of forgetting them on purpose?"

"You tell me? You're the one who was trying to trap me."

"Is that how you see this, Alek?" she practically spits out. "Or should I say, Aleksander Ivanov."

I flinch like she'd just slapped me and in a sense, she did. "That is my name. I shortened it, and my middle name is Mikhail, so I just went with Alek Hail," I explain.

"I guess I wasn't the only one hiding my identity, was I?"

I rip the bowtie off my neck and toss it to the floor. "I had reasons. You see who my family is. I never told you because half the women run the other way when they find out where I come from, and the other half want money or something from me when they realize I'm an Ivanov. Look at what

Chase's mother did. She took half of what I owned and took off, never to be heard from again."

"I guess you think I fall into the latter half of those women." She removes her veil and tosses it away. "You paid my tuition, and figured I'd gotten what I wanted and therefore had no reason to stick around."

"I'm not saying....look. You tried to trap me into falling for you and marrying you. Did you think this was the only way to get me to the altar? I *was* falling for you, Anna. Correction, I'd fallen for you. If you would have hung around, I would have told you that and I would have asked you to marry me."

She shakes her head like she doesn't believe a word I'm saying. "I heard you, Alek. The night I left, I heard you on the phone making plans with your mother."

My mind goes blank for a second, and I take a deep breath. "She was planning a birthday party for Chase in her gardens. I wanted a small party at our house—I mean, *my* house—but she insisted on a party planner and a big bash. I hate that shit, but agreed because it was easier, especially when I was trying to get her off my back about getting married. I've learned what to fight for and what not to fight for."

"Yeah, and I'm not worth fighting for, clearly."

"You're the one who was tricking me," I say, and even as the words fall off my tongue, I realize there's a sour taste to them, and they don't sound right, not even to my ears.

Her shoulders sag a bit, a new kind of weariness about her. "That's what you think of me? After everything, that's what you think I'd do, Alek?" She shakes her head, dumbfounded, exasperated...heartbroken.

She stares at me, a deep sadness in her eyes. It curls around me, has me questioning everything. Was I wrong?

I cover my face with my hands as my throat squeezes tight. I work to sort through everything, and one thing keeps gnawing at me. "I don't believe in coincidences. You know that." Chicago is a big city. How is it, she landed at my neighbors, and then at my place, if that wasn't all planned? It makes no sense.

"I actually don't believe in coincidences either, but I'm smart enough to ask questions before jumping to conclusions and dishing out accusations, but it's nice to know what you really think of me. Oh, and yes, I know you like honesty, so let me be completely honest with you. I wasn't trying to trap you. The morning after we had sex without a condom, I went looking for a morning after pill."

I open my mouth to ask why she didn't tell me, but she continues with, "I probably should have told you, but I thought I could take care of things myself, and I didn't want to ruin what was blossoming between us, nor did I want to risk a pregnancy, or take a chance that down the road that you'd accuse me of trapping you. Which is exactly what you're doing anyway."

"You should have told me."

"You're probably right, and I'm sorry. But it sure is clear to me that you don't know me at all."

"I...Christ. I don't know what to think, what to believe...You just left."

"One of my father's men came to your house the night I left. He gave me an ultimatum. I leave quietly with him, or I risk him hurting you and Chase. You don't have to believe anything I say, Alek. But you should probably believe this." She holds her index finger up. "One, I'm not pregnant. Thank God, because I wouldn't want to bring your child into the world and have him turn out like you." Her middle finger joins her index. "Two, I will pay you back every cent you paid for me to go to culinary school." Her bare ring finger joins the other two. "And three, I never want to see you again."

I swallow around the lump in my throat. God, what have I done? I sit there, my legs like lead beneath me as she opens the door and walks out on me. She's right. I should have asked questions. Maybe she had nothing to do with finding herself working at Theresa's place. From the guilt on Theresa's face, they were in on it, but that doesn't mean Anna was the one manipulating the circumstances. I should have asked instead of accused.

I can't blame her for being angry, or walking out, never wanting to see me again. Past experiences had me acting out, expecting the worst of her, when in fact she's nothing like the conniving woman who married me, took what she wanted and left without warning.

I bend forward, rest my elbows on my legs, and my head in my palms. She never wants to see me again. The woman I'm in love with, the girl my son loves, is gone—not that I blame her—and there isn't a goddamn thing I can do about it.

Or can I?

21

ANNA

I walk out of the small, stifling room, and all eyes turn to me as I stand at the front of the church, black mascara running down my face. I swipe at it, but what do I care what any of these people think. With a fistful of dress in my palms, I force my feet to move, smooth and steady, one in front of the other, and head straight for the closed double doors, needing air before I pass out in front of all the people staring at me—judging me. The hell with them all. They have no idea that I just had my heart and soul ripped from my body.

A palm lands on my shoulder and for a second I think it's Alek, wanting me to turn around so he can tell me he's made a big mistake. Would I even forgive him? After all we shared, all we've been through, does he really think I'm the type of girl who would trick and manipulate him for my own benefit. It was just a couple weeks ago, under the cover of darkness, that I left quietly to protect him and his son, going back to a home where I was stifled, my life ruled, to keep him safe, even after I heard him making plans for a backyard wedding.

Yes, okay, I was mistaken about that, but I still wanted to protect him. I shake my head, my tears heavy in my eyes. He obviously doesn't know me at all.

"Anna."

I spin and my father's hand falls from my shoulder. His eyes hold a measure of sorrow and guilt, but it's nothing compared to the hurt in my heart.

"What?" I ask through clenched teeth, not really wanting a conversation with him in front of an audience.

"Where are you going?"

Really? He's asking where I'm going after what just took place. An almost hysterical laugh bubbles in my throat as understanding rushes through my brain.

"You set this all up, didn't you?" I ask.

His brow furrows and he takes a measured step closer, his words for my ears only. "I didn't think things would go down like this."

"How did you think they'd go down?"

"I thought once you saw it was Aleksander, you'd be thrilled."

I briefly close my eyes before I lose it entirely. "Why would I be thrilled?"

He glances over his shoulder, but Alek isn't rushing from the back room to proclaim his love for me. It's over between us. "Because you'd...fallen in love with him."

"And you know that because you were aware of my every movement since I left home, right?" I'm aware of the eyes on me and I'm not usually a girl to cause a scene, but I can't help myself. I need answers. "You knew about the nanny agency, I take it?" So much for thinking burner phones were going to help.

"I knew what you were up to, yes."

I at least appreciate his honesty. "You arranged for me to be placed with Theresa and Gio." I scan the crowd, and Theresa has her head down, like she's praying. I shake my own head as she avoids my gaze.

"They're good people, Anna." His voice is gruff, but there's also something else there, something that sounds like worry. He should be worried. I don't ever plan on talking to him again. "Don't be angry with them."

"I should only be angry with you then?"

"This isn't what I wanted. I wanted...for you to be happy with a man who will always put your needs and best interests first."

My heart pinches. "No, what you wanted was for me to be Sophie's nanny, to have Theresa fire me in front of Alek, and then for Alek to take me in, like I was a stray animal or something, and then with any luck, we'd fall for each other and get married. A marriage that brings two families together, and that's what you wanted all along. My happiness had nothing to do with this." A tortured cry lodges in my throat. "Well done, Dad. You got everything you wanted...except the wedding. It's not happening today, or ever. The two families will have to find another way to come together."

He reaches for me. "Anna—"

"Don't." I pull back from him, and gasps fill the silence of the church. "What I want to know is why Bruno forced me to return home. Why not leave me there, leaving us none the wiser to your ploy?"

A scowl moves over his face. "Bruno messed up. You weren't supposed to see him."

"He's like three hundred pounds. Hard to miss someone like that, don't you think? But I still don't get it."

My father scans the crowd and I follow his gaze when it lands on Bruno. He's standing tall at the back of the church, keeping guard, but he squirms a bit as Dad zeroes in on him. "He panicked, and figured you'd run away again after you saw him. He couldn't risk that happening, so he brought you back home to me."

"Why didn't you just tell me everything then? Why wait until..." I look around the church. "...this?"

"You were dead set against marrying a man of my choosing—even though I knew that man was perfect for you—and I figured if I told you I was behind you and Aleksander meeting, you would have revolted, and maybe run again. I thought once you saw him here, realized how much you loved him, all would be right in the world."

"Well, Dad, all is not right in the world. If it was, I'd be in culinary school, traveling, seeing Paris, and experiencing life, and then falling in love. I never needed a man in my life, Dad." At least Alek realized that, and encouraged me to follow my dreams.

Before he can say anything else, I turn and run out of the church, tears pouring down my face. I run down the sidewalk, weaving in and out of people as they gawk at me. I continue to run, with nowhere to go, no one to turn to. I don't even have money for a cab ride. As I run, and the sidewalk blurs before my eyes, a female voice calls out to me. I slow and a car pulls up next to me. Oh great, it's mean girl Chloe from high school. She's going to love seeing me like this. I'm sure I'll be all over social media within seconds.

"Anna, are you okay?" she asks, her eyes narrowed, and I spot real sincerity there.

"No, I'm not okay."

She slams her car into park, jumps from the driver's seat and comes around to me. She puts her arm around my shoulders, and I let her lead me to the passenger seat. I drop in, and she reaches around me to buckle me in.

A moment later, she's back in the driver's seat and I stare straight ahead, not knowing or caring where she's taking me. After a good long drive, she pulls up to The Parker, a luxury apartment building in Chicago's West Loop.

"Is this where you live?" I ask.

"Yes, and now it's where you live, too. Until you figure some things out."

I sniff. "Why?"

"Come on, Anna. Let's go inside and talk."

She parks in her spot and helps me from the car in my ridiculously big wedding gown that I let my mother pick out for me. I didn't want to have anything to do with the wedding. I didn't care.

I wipe my tears and work to pull myself together as she guides me to her floor. Inside, I make my way to the window and take in the breathtaking view of the city.

"Gorgeous," I say. I turn to her, curious. Her parents are wealthy, and no doubt paying for this, but I can't help but wonder what else she's been doing since we graduated. "Are you still working at the lingerie store?"

"Yes, but I'm going to college as well."

"Nice," I say. "What are you taking?"

"Psychology." She taps the sofa. "Come sit."

I plunk down next to her. "I'm signed up for culinary school, winter session."

"You'll be an amazing chef."

I pluck at my dress. "Why are you being so nice to me?"

She gives a humorless laugh. "I did a lot of work on myself after graduation. I was mean to you, and I'm sorry about that, Anna. Deep down I was jealous."

I give a humorless laugh. "What could you possibly be jealous about?"

"I thought you had it all. The life, the looks, the body. I never stopped to think about what life was like for you." She touches my dress. "I'm guessing it's not been so great, huh?"

"I need to get out of this."

"Come on, we're the same size. You can tell me all about it as you get changed."

I follow her to her room, and twenty minutes later, I'm in a comfy pair of sweats and a T-shirt back on the sofa.

"That's pretty shitty, Anna," Chloe says, a frown on her face. "I thought Alek was your bodyguard when I ran into you two. I didn't realize he was more. I wasn't trying to be mean when I ran into you. In fact, I wanted to apologize."

"Thank you." I glance out the window, and my heart breaks. Alek was more than a protector. He was kind, and caring, putting my needs first. God, he was so patient taking my virginity, preparing me, taking his time so he could do right by me. How could a man like that think I was so cold and calculating?

"You really love him, don't you?"

The tears start again, and I bury my face in my hands. "I do."

"Tell me more about him."

I laugh when I think how he caved and got Chase a turtle. "He's strong and domineering..." I put my hand over my heart. "But in here, he's kind of a softie."

Chloe smiles at me. "He sounds sweet."

"Yeah, he is. Or at least, I thought he was." I look away. "He has this ridiculous to-do list in a jar. Sometimes he puts fun things in there for the nanny to do, though."

"Such as?"

I shrug. "Take his son, Chase to the park. Get ice cream. Sleep in. Things like that. He's so good with Chase."

"What happened to Chase's mother?"

"She left him. She nearly cleaned him out, and left both Alek and Chase behind. Who does something like that?"

"Someone horrible." She goes quiet, and I can almost hear her brain spinning.

"What?"

"Maybe that's why he reacted the way he did? I mean, past experiences, preconceived notions, flaws...they influence our perspective, especially under times of stress." She takes my hand. "Tell me more about Alek and Chase."

I start to talk, and the words rush out. I tell her about our time fishing, and cooking and visiting his neighbors. I tell her about culinary school and how he fought for me because he wanted me to succeed, and the more I talk, and the more my heart aches, the more I realize that Alek might have been acting out of fear, out of past experiences. He was afraid. There was always a vulnerability about him, a need for him to be and feel loved and needed.

Oh, God, did I make a huge mistake, telling him I never wanted to see him again?

After talking for hours on end, Chloe puts her hand over her mouth and yawns.

"I'm sorry for keeping you up so long."

"Don't be," she says. "And once again, I'm sorry for what happened in high school. Home life wasn't great and I was insecure and jealous and trying to navigate life. I'm in a much better place now." Her smile is soft, warm and welcoming, "Now that you understand where I was coming from and what I was going through, do you forgive me?"

I nod. "I do." I smile at Chloe, and like the idea of the two of us being friends. I know I sure could use one.

"Thank you." She glances at her watch and we both yawn. It's been a very long day and night, and I definitely need sleep. Tomorrow is a new day, a new beginning and I somehow have to find a way to move forward, without Alek and Chase in my life. "Forgiveness is important, don't you think?" Chloe asks.

My throat squeezes tight. "It is important." Alek accused me of some pretty horrible things, and even if he realizes his mistake, realizes none of those things were true, there's no way we could be together. Not after the cruel things I shot back at him—out of anger and fear, much like he did. God, I told him I'd never want a child who was anything like him, that I never want to see him again.

There's no way on the face of this earth he'd ever forgive me.

ALEK

"What do you mean you don't know where she is?" I ask the private investigator as I pace around my house and press my phone harder against my ear.

"There's no sign of her, Alek."

"It's been a week and nothing?" I pace to my window and glance out at the backyard. With Chase at school, the yard, as well as the house, is as empty as my heart. I can't work. I can't sleep, and I definitely can't eat. All I can do, is worry about Anna and the horrible way we parted.

I never should have let her walk out of the church that day. I should have gone after her. The truth is, in my heart I knew she needed time to deal with what her father had done to her, not to mention the horrible things I said to her—accused her of. I'll never forgive myself for that and now I can't even find her to apologize or beg for forgiveness.

Honestly though, how could she have just disappeared? She left the church in her wedding gown, and nothing else. She had no money to leave Chicago, which means she must still be here. She has to be right, but where? I've gone everywhere, from the grocery stores in our neighborhood, to the culinary school, to roaming the streets, but she up and disappeared without a trace.

A knock sounds on my door. "I have to go. Please, keep looking." I rush down the hall, praying it's Anna. I pull open the front door and stare at a girl I've never met before. My heart drops to my stomach, disappointment hitting like a fist to the face. The girl stands there staring at me, shifting from one foot to the other. Wait, do I know her?

"Hi," she says.

"Hi."

"Um, it's possible I'm overstepping, but I can't stand to see Anna hurting."

My pulse leaps into my throat and I reach out and grab the girl's arm, afraid she might flee. "You know Anna?"

"Uh…" She glances at my hand, and the death grip I have on her.

I let her go and hold my hands up, palms out. "I'm sorry. I shouldn't have touched you. It's…just. Anna. I'm so worried about her."

"She's okay." She frowns. "Sort of. Well, no, that's not entirely true. She's not okay."

My throat dries, and a groan slips from my lips as the world spins out on me. "Please tell me. Where is she? I need to talk to her."

"I know you do. That's why I'm here. Overstepping."

Something niggles loose in the back of my brain, and my gaze moves over her face. Recognition hits. "You're the girl we ran into at the lingerie shop."

"That's me." She holds her hand out. "I'm Chloe."

"I don't understand. I didn't think you and Anna were friends. How do you know where she is?"

"We are now. I saw her running down the street in her wedding gown and I took her home with me. She's been staying at my place."

"Thank God." I shake my head, a measure of relief soaring through my blood to know Anna is safe. "Thank you."

She shifts from one foot to the other. "I think you two need to talk."

I glance over her shoulder, and look at her vehicle, but it's empty. "I've been looking for her."

"She's worried that you hate her for the things she said to you."

"She's the one who hates me, and rightfully so. I am such an idiot."

"She doesn't hate you, Alek."

"Can you take me to her?" I plead and I've never pleaded for anything in my life. Nothing was ever worth pleading for until now. "Where is she?" She glances over her shoulder, like she's worried that she's giving too much away. "I love her, Chloe. I love her more than life itself. I want to marry her. I want her to be Chase's mother. I want to give her everything she's ever wanted."

She nods, and her eyes fill with tears. "That's so sweet." She looks around again. "Today is the first day I was able to get her to leave the condo. She's actually at Grant Park. I drove her there, and told her I had errands to run. She's there until I pick her up."

I'm already rushing through the house and grabbing everything I need, and locking up by the time she finishes telling me where I can find Anna.

"Uh, what's that for?" she asks when she sees what I'm holding in my hand.

"It's a long story. But thank you, Chloe. I owe you big time."

"Nah, I'm just happy to help and maybe make up for things I did in my past."

I jump into my car, back out of the driveway quickly and head straight for Grant Park. "Breathe, Alek, breathe," I say to myself as my heart races and I grow lightheaded. I finally make it to my destination and have to circle forever to find a parking spot. I think about shooting a text off to Anna to ask where she is, but I don't want to give her a heads up. She might run.

I finally find a parking spot, and gather up the stuff I brought from the house. I speed walk through the park, and the second I see the woman I'm in love with on a bench reading, I just about drop to my knees and sob. My throat squeezes as tears pound behind my eyes, and nervousness has me slowing my steps. I can barely breathe when I finally reach her, and it's not from walking fast. I stand over her, blocking the sun.

Her head lifts, a frown on her face, but her eyes go wide when she sees it's me standing there. She stiffens and tries to push back further into the bench, like she wants to run, or is worried that I'm going to lash out again.

"Anna," I begin. I swallow, and take a few breaths to pull myself together. I don't want to fuck this up. "I've been looking everywhere for you."

"You found me," she answers, sounding as breathless and shaky as I do.

"I'm so sorry. I'm so goddamn sorry for the things I said, the things I accused you of..." I shake my head, and gulp air. "My past, my ex...you're nothing like her. I shouldn't have, for one second, thought you were trying to manipulate me. That's not you. You're the kindest, most caring woman I know. Our meeting wasn't a coincidence, I realize that now, and I don't care how we met. Meeting you was the best thing that ever happened to me, and I know you're likely not talking to your father, and what he did was wrong. What my parents did was wrong. But I'm thankful every day they brought us together."

She sniffs. "Alek, I'm sorry. I wanted to come to you. I was worried...I just..."

She's going to give me a chance.

Relief washes through me, and I can barely fill my lungs with air. I hold my hand up to cut her off. "Please don't say anything more. Not yet." I drop to my knees in front of her, and hold out my to-do jar. Her head jerks back.

"What...what is that for?"

"It's a to-do list, just for you."

Her brow furrows, and my heart pounds faster. "I don't understand."

I open the lid, and pull out the sheet with the number one on it. I hand it to her. "Please read this out loud."

Her eyes are full of confusion as they leave mine to focus on the paper and she begins, "My jet is at the airport ready to take you anywhere in the world. Get on it, go to Paris like you've always wanted. Go anywhere you want." She blinks at me, and I pull out the sheet with number two on it.

She reads it. "Apply to the Culinary Institute of America in New York." A small smile tugs at the corners of her mouth as I reach in and grab sheet number three.

"Do all the things you want to do, see all the things you want to see, live the life you've always wanted to live and find your-self before you settle down into marriage." I hand her sheet number four.

"After you do all those things, will you go on a date with me?" She smiles, and tears fall down her face. "Yes, Alek, I will."

My heart soars as I hand her sheet number five, and once again I find myself holding my breath because this is a big one.

She reads it. "After that date, maybe you will think about being my wife, and Chase's mother?" She chokes on the words and takes deep gulping breaths. I shimmy closer, and put one hand on her leg.

"Anna."

"No," she says and shoves the notes into my chest.

I falter backward a bit, the park spinning before my eyes. I can't lose her. "No?"

"No." she takes a big deep breath, and a cold chill goes through me as I watch her. Is this it? Is it really over between us? I'm about to ask when she says, "It's my turn to talk." She glances at the jar. "I appreciate all this, Alek. I appreciate you wanting me to use your jet to see the world, to go to school in New York, to live the life I missed out on, and to find myself, but I'm not doing any of those things."

"Why...not?" I managed to get out.

"Because none of them will mean anything to me if I'm not doing them with you." A big ugly sob catches in my throat as she puts her hands on my face. "I love you. When I get on your private jet, I want us to be going away on our honeymoon in Paris. When I go to culinary school, I want to go here, so I can make meals for you and Chase every night, and I don't need to go anywhere to live life or find myself. I've lived life and found myself here, with you. I was wrong when I told my father, I didn't need a man."

"You were?"

"Yes, I was. I need you, Alek. I need you in my life and my bed..." She chuckles. "You're already in my heart and in my head, and I wouldn't want it any other way. But I want everything, the rest. All of you." Her gaze moves over my face, and her eyes turn serious. "I never meant—"

I lean in and kiss her, swallowing her apology. We hold onto one another like our lives depend on it and she cries into my shoulder as I pull her to me—but this time they're happy tears.

She inches back, and I ask, "Do you have a pen?"

Confusion dances in her blue eyes. "What?"

"A pen, please."

"Ah, no, sorry I don't."

"I do," a voice says from behind and we turn to find Chloe standing there. She hands me a pen and smiles at Anna.

"You were behind this," Anna says quietly, a statement, not an accusation.

"I hope you're not mad."

"I'm not. Thank you."

As the women talk, I scribble a new note to Anna. She turns back to me. "Since you're not going to do any of the other things in my to-do jar, maybe this is the only paper that should have been in there." I hand it to her, and she reads it.

"Marry me. Make me the happiest man in the world."

She glances up at me. "Say yes," I plead.

"Yes." I jump up, pull her up with me and spin her around. When I finally stop, she frowns, and asks, "Should we tell our parents?"

I shake my head. "Nah, I think maybe we should let them sweat it out a bit longer."

She laughs and I kiss her again. "I think you're right."

"Get a room already," Chloe teases.

"Speaking of sweating things out..." I say with a wink.

Chloe points to the entrance to the park. "Ohmigod, go."

As we both laugh, I scoop her into my arms. "Before we get that room, there's one thing we need to do," she informs me, all humor gone from her face.

I search my brain, but for the life of me I can't figure out what she means. "What?"

"We need to go to Chase's school and tell him he's getting a new mommy."

My heart swells in my chest, and everything I feel for this woman rises to the surface and fills my soul with so much love I nearly sink to my knees. "Thank you, Anna. He's going to love that."

"Good, because I love that little boy as much as I love his father."

"I love that little boy as much as I love his nanny," I say in return and we both laugh as I carry her out of the park and into our new life.

EPILOGUE

Anna

One Year Later:

Standing inside our cottage at the lake, the breeze blowing in through the open windows, I take a deep breath of the warm afternoon air and listen to the birds chirping in the distance. A grin pulls at my face when I hear our dog Charlie, a beautiful Bernese Mountain dog, bark. No doubt he's chasing after the birds or a bunny. Or maybe he's in the water, trying to catch a fish. Another one of his favorite pastimes. My heart is so full as I glance out at the decorated dock, where my fiancé and his son are waiting for me.

"Are you ready?" Debra asks as she adjusts my veil.

I blink back the tears, not wanting to ruin my makeup, but I'm having a heck of a time keeping all my emotions in check. "I've been ready for a full year now."

Chloe laughs and claps her hands with happiness. "You look so gorgeous, Anna. I couldn't be happier for you." I turn and face the mirror. Today, unlike my last botched wedding to the man I love, I'm wearing a gown of my choice. I take in the pretty white dress. It's a simple off the shoulder satin dress, one that Chloe and my mother helped me pick out and it's perfect for a lakeside wedding.

I turn to Debra and take her hands in mine. "I can't thank you enough. The place is gorgeous. I could never have pulled together something so simple, yet elegant." We hired Debra to decorate for us and she did the most amazing job by stringing up lights everywhere, decorating the chairs with ribbons, and the dining tables are set with elegant gold candlesticks and foliage. There's an arch of flowers I will walk through to get to the dock and there are large white pillar candles everywhere, making everything so stylish. The candles will be lit tonight as we dance under the stars. She even thought of a white, billowy outdoor canopy that will keep the rain out, but allow light in. Fortunately, it's a sunny day.

She smiles at the compliment. "I think Nick is old enough now that I can turn my hobby into a career."

"Glad to hear that." I lean in and whisper, "We might need a nursery decorated soon."

Both women squeal in delight, and I can hardly stop smiling. Alek and I want another child, but he was worried it would interfere with school. I'm pretty sure, with a little help, and he's always there to help, we can juggle it all.

After a round of hugs, I smile as the two women who've become my closest friends over the last year fuss over me. One year ago, I had no one, and now I have Alek, Chase, Chloe, Debra, her husband Jack, and son Nick. I have Theresa and Gio, my old employers—yes, Alek and I forgave them—and their daughter Sophie. I also have my family. Mom, Dad and I had a long talk, and there was lots of understanding on their part, and more forgiveness by Alek and myself.

Outside the music changes and a giggle bubbles up in my throat as I remember Alek on his knees with his to-do jar. Could the man be any sweeter? He proved he knew me well, and while he encouraged me to go to New York because it was my dream—at least I let him believe it was—I made the decision to stay here for school, and now I have the first year under my belt. I've loved being home every night cooking for my guys, and soon enough, we'll be putting another seat at our table. Or rather, a highchair.

"Let's go," Chloe says, and she picks up her flowers and starts out of the house. Before she leaves, I catch her arm, lean in and give her a kiss on the cheek.

"Love you," I say. "Thank you for everything."

"Love you too, Anna." She smiles and heads outside. Debra follows her and so do I. I step into the sunshine, and my dad is standing there at the door waiting for me.

"You look beautiful," he tells me, and I'm pretty sure he has tears in his eyes. A man like him never shows weakness or emotions, so I know this wedding is as big a deal for him as it was for me.

"I love him, Dad. I love him with all my heart."

"I know you do. You couldn't have asked for a better man."

"I guess you knew that all along, huh?"

He gives me a sheepish grin. "Let's not keep him waiting, then."

I meet Mom's gaze, and her love reaches out to me. I smile at her, giving her all my gratitude as Dad and I walk toward the dock. Things weren't always good between us, but in my heart, I know my best interests were first and foremost with them. They just have a strange way of showing it.

My pulse pounds harder in my throat when I spot my best friend, my lover, the man I am going to spend the rest of my life with, looking so handsome in his tux, anxiously waiting for me. As a hush grows over the crowd, Alek and I share a private smile, and I force myself to walk slowly when all I want to do is rush to him.

"Mommy," Chase screams and we all laugh. He started calling me that the day we went to his school to tell him, and the paperwork has been submitted for my official adoption of him.

"Hey little man," I say and his freshly cleaned face glows with happiness as he stands proudly in his tux, glancing up at his amazing father.

We stop before we reach Alek and Dad removes my veil and kisses my cheek. He goes back to the lawn and takes a seat with the rest of the guests. There aren't many. We wanted to keep it simple and elegant. I walk through the flower archway and stand beside Alek.

"I'm the luckiest man in the world," Alek says when I reach him.

"Yeah, you are," I tease with a wink, the warm breeze billowing my dress.

He laughs, and I laugh with him. Before I realize what's happening, he leans in and kisses me. Our guests laugh and the minister says, "Um, we haven't gotten to that part yet."

Alek takes my hands in his, as the minister asks us to recite our vows after him. I recite mine and when he turns to Alek, he holds his hand up and declares, "I wrote my own."

"You did?" I ask, shocked and touched by the gesture. He turns, bends down and grabs his to-do jar, and I can't help but laugh. "Alek, what did you do?"

He grins at me, pulls out a long sheet of paper and hands the empty jar to our son. He unfolds the paper. "These are the things I plan to do for the rest of our lives." My heart overflows with love as he begins, "I plan to support you in whatever you do, whether that's working for a restaurant or owning your own. I plan to always be there for you, in the good times and the bad. I plan to be an honest, faithful, and loving husband for the rest of our lives. I plan to stand with you and beside you. I plan to be your husband and your best friend. I'm a better man when I'm with you, Anna, and I'm the luckiest guy in the world to call you mine."

Tears flow down my face when he finishes, and the second the minister announces us husband and wife, I go up on my toes to kiss the man I love more than anything in this world. Alek turns me, ready to walk to our family and friends and enjoy a lovely afternoon of wine, food and dancing.

"Wait," I say.

"I've waited long enough," Alek mutters with a laugh. "I guess another minute won't hurt." He brushes the back of his hand along my cheek. "What is it, love?"

I reach around one of the big flowerpots and grab the jar I stashed there earlier. "You're not the only one with a to-do jar, Alek."

"What did you do?" he asks using my words and grinning from ear to ear as our guests laugh with pleasure. I take the lid off, pull out a small piece of paper and set the jar on the dock. I hand it to him. "Read it to yourself first."

He eyes me suspiciously, then glances down. His smile falls, and his dark eyes go wide with wonderment and joy. I stand there restlessly, shifting from one foot to the other, unable to contain my excitement. His head lifts and his eyes are stormy when they meet mine. I couldn't love him any more than I do at this moment.

"Really?"

I nod. "Really." He gathers me up, and spins me around, and once I'm back on my feet he goes down on his knees to put one arm around his son. He glances out at our guests, and reads the paper.

"Anna's list of things to do: Be the best wife to my husband, and the best mom to our children. Our little family is growing, Alek."

Everyone goes quiet for a second, until I put my hand on my stomach. Gio jumps up and screams, "The rabbit died," which is a very old-fashioned way of saying someone is pregnant. Everyone claps, and Alek stands and hugs me.

"Thank you, Anna. You have given me everything I've ever wanted."

I touch my stomach, and can't wait for it to grow. "You sort of had a hand in this."

His head dips, and his lips are close to mine. "Let's go celebrate," he says, his voice soft, passionate, full of love.

"Daddy, I want a rabbit," Chase blurts out and as we laugh again. Alek bends and gathers our son into his arms.

"Can we talk about that later, little man," he says, and I smile up at my husband because I know in the near future, our house will not only have a turtle and a dog, it will also have a baby and a rabbit, and I can't wait.

***

Thank you so much for reading, **Hot Nanny Next Door**, book 4 in my Single Dad Series. I hope you loved this story as much as I loved writing it.

If you love mistaken identity romance, check out Away Game, book on in my Scotia Storms Series.

Chase:

I know we get bad storms in Boston, but come on, this is ridiculous. I lean forward and peer out my icy window, but I can barely see two feet in front of my Jeep. My wipers are on high, yet they're unable to keep up with the heavy flakes coating my window. Everything from my vehicle to the road and trees are covered in inches of thick, wet snow, making this journey treacherous, and nearly impossible.

I drive by a sign on this narrow back road in Nova Scotia, but it's whited out and unreadable. Even if the words were visible, I'm not from around these parts, so it wouldn't mean much to me. Still, I'd like to at least know my whereabouts, should

I go flying off some cliff and somehow—miraculously—survive.

Seriously though, I have no idea where I am, or if this winding road leads to Halifax. Christ, I've never heard of the Trans-Canada highway shutting down before, the four-lane freeway completely impassable, forcing drivers to take these backwoods detours. Then again, I've never been in stormy Nova Scotia during the dead of winter either.

If I had it my way, I'd be back in Boston at the dorm, getting ready to fly home for three days, for a short break before we gear up for the playoffs, but I had no choice in the matter. This is the only time I could join the Scotia Storms for practice and decide whether I want to stay and play hockey at Boston University or join the Storms, a top Atlantic university hockey team in Halifax.

My buddy Brandon raves about the Scotia Storms—now I see where they get their name—and the top-notch education at the Academy. He says the downtown nightlife has a great vibe, with genuine people, and the city, by far, has the hottest women on the planet. I don't really believe that. I think it's just his way to lure me here. Although Brandon would never lie to me. The two of us go way back to our kindergarten years. Our dads played together for the Seattle Shooters, and yes, we both feel the pressure that comes with our father's high levels of achievement.

But speaking of Brandon, he could have at least warned me that the roads were going to be deadly. Last I heard there were over fifteen-hundred vehicles stranded on the Trans-Canada. Shit, he probably thinks I'm one of them and is no doubt worried sick. No way can I take my hands off the wheel or eyes off the road to message him and I don't dare pull over in these conditions. It's a total white out. I can't even tell where the road ends and the ditch begins. Not that I think I'd have service out here in the middle of nowhere—and yes, it's true, I'm the only idiot on this particular back road.

I grip the steering wheel tighter and blink, trying not to get snow hypnosis and veer into a tree. I turn my high beams on and off. It does nothing to help with my visibility. The road curves and I ease off the gas to coast around the turn. From my peripheral vision, I spot movement and shoot a fast glance to my right. What the hell was that? I adjust my rearview mirror and catch a flash of something...or someone. I pinch my eyes shut and open them again. I must be imagining things. No one would be standing on the side of the road in the middle of a storm...unless.

I slow to a stop, and back up. My tires spin the whole way, and when I see movement again, I shove my Jeep into park and hop out. My boots sink into the snow, slowing me down. I circle my vehicle and that's when I realize there's a car in the ditch, and my spraying tires just soaked someone standing a few feet away from the vehicle's flashing brake lights. I quickly take in his splayed arms, and the way he's gasping as slush drips from his winter coat.

"Are you okay?" I yell, but my words get carried away in the wind. I step closer to the motionless figure, and come face to face with Frosty the Snowman. Technically it's a person, but all that's missing to complete the children's beloved character is the carrot nose. You know what's not missing? The eyes made out of coal. Yeah, that's right. This guy has two black eyes peering out from a snowy hood tugged tight and if looks could kill I'd be a goner. I'm guessing he's not about to come to life and spread good cheer. Can't say I blame him. "I'm sorry. I didn't mean to soak you."

"It's okay. It's not your fault, but dammit, isn't this day just getting better and better," the guy—or rather the girl—says as fat snowflakes coat her lashes.

My gaze races over her shivering body, as she shifts from one foot to the other. She's all bundled up so I can't tell if she's injured from the crash. "Are you hurt?"

She wraps her arms around herself and her breath turns to fog as she speaks. "No, just cold and wet and late."

I understand late. I pull my phone from my pocket to check for service. Zilch. Not only that, I'm down to one bar. "Do you have service?"

"No. I can't even call for a tow truck, and the closest town is a few miles down the road. I don't think I can make it on foot."

At least one of us knows where we are. I'm grateful for that. I shake my head as a cold shiver goes through me. "Here I thought I was the only idiot on this side road."

"Did you just call me an idiot?"

"What, no." Way to make a first good impression, Chase. "I didn't mean that. I'm the idiot. I should have turned back instead of taking the detour." I gesture with a nod to my Jeep. "You'd better get in and we need to get off the road before someone takes that corner too fast and crashes into us."

"I..." She glances at the tail end of her car sticking out of the ditch, the brake lights fading to black. She groans and looks back at me. It's easy to tell she's not comfortable climbing into a car with a stranger. I don't blame her.

"I'm not a serial killer," I say, hoping to ease her worries.

"Which is exactly what a serial killer would say, but under the circumstances, I'm safer with you than in this storm." She eyes me for a second, like she's committing my features to memory. "Just so you know, I know judo."

I hold my hands up, palms out. "Duly noted."

I shuffle my feet in the snow to make a path for her, and she follows me to the passenger side. I open the door, and a burst of snow follows her in. My gaze moves over her for a second. How the hell did I think she was a guy? She's so petite, it's a surprise her feet reach the floor. Once she's secure, I trudge through the wet snow again and climb into the driver's side, cranking up the heat to melt the snow covering her coat.

She tugs off her mitts and holds her quivering hands over the vents to warm them, and I resist the urge to take them in mine and create heat with friction. That would be inappropriate, and something tells me she'd judo me right in the nuts.

"I am so cold." I flick on the heated seat and after a few moments, she wiggles. "Oh, that is so nice."

As soon as we're both buckled up, I cast her a quick glance. "Ready?"

She nods, and I glance around to make sure the road is clear behind me before I hit the gas. My wipers squeal as they struggle with the snow and I lean forward to concentrate on the road. "How far did you say the next town was?"

"Just a couple miles. Not much there, but there is a gas station, and a small motel. It could be full, or shut down. Storms like these tend to knock out the power for days."

Shit. "I don't have days." I had plans to join the guys on the ice and check out the academy's curriculum to figure out if I want to pack up my life in Boston and move to Canada. By the looks of things right now, I'm going to miss a few days that I can't afford to miss. The coach isn't going to want a guy on the team who can't show up on time. I just hope Brandon talks to him and can postpone our meeting.

"Me neither." She groans and looks out the window.

"What are you late for?"

"I was meeting a friend Lily in New Brunswick and tomorrow we're supposed to fly to Florida for the holidays. Her parents have a place there." A shiver goes through her as the cold leaves her body. "I was so looking forward to the warm weather."

"Warm weather would be nice right about now."

She takes a deep breath and lets it out slowly as she looks in the side view mirror. "I suppose it could be worse. I could have died in the crash."

"Hey, way to look on the bright side." She turns and practically snarls at me. I bite back a grin. "Too soon?"

"Too soon," she says and grumbles something about her father warning her about the weather and how she was sure she could beat the snow and that I was right—she's is an idiot.

"They weren't calling for this much snow, which is why I decided to drive to New Brunswick and fly out with Lily," she explains like she's trying to justify her actions.

"Meteorologists," I tease. "The only thing they get right is it's light today and dark tonight."

She chuckles at that, and the sweet sound wraps around me.

"True, but the weather can be unpredictable here in Nova Scotia this time of year."

I think it's sweet that she's standing up for the meteorologists, especially after veering off the road. My heart softens as I take in her disappointment. "I'm sorry you're missing your trip. Can you reschedule for Monday? Catch another flight?"

She laughs, almost manically. Maybe I should be the one worried about her being the serial killer.

"You're obviously not from around here."

"Boston," I state, and when she arches a brow, I continue with, "I'm meeting a buddy in Halifax for the February break." I don't bother telling her who I am and the real reason I'm heading to the city. People instantly change when they find out my father was in the NHL, and that I'm his little prodigy who is expected to live up to the hype. I hate it, all of it. The expectation. The girls who want me because I play hockey. I can never tell who's real and who isn't, who likes me because I can sink a puck, and who likes me just for me. It's honestly kind of nice chatting with someone who has no idea who I really am.

All that will change when I reach the city—I'll be introduced around as Chase Adams, a lightning fast forward with great leadership skills, drafted at eighteen and expected to head to the NHL after college. But for right now, I'd like to be incognito and maybe we can just be two strangers who don't have to know anything about each other and can become friends. Although that's a bit ridiculous. I probably won't set eyes on her again.

She nods. "If you were from around here, you'd know that it's going to take days to get plowed out, especially up here on the mountain."

I nod. I thought I was climbing on this back road, but it was hard to tell. "My name is Chase," I tell her, not bothering to tell her my recognizable last name. Then again, Adams is a common name and she might not put two and two together and realize Jamie Adams, former player for the Seattle Shooters, is my father.

"Nice to meet you, Chase. I'm Sawyer." I note that she doesn't bother giving me her last name either. I've never met a girl named Sawyer before, and I dig the name. "I'd shake your hand, but I don't want you to take yours off the wheel."

"Good call." She goes quiet for a second and I can almost feel the disappointment rolling off her.

"I'm glad you're not hurt, and your car didn't look too banged up. It's probably still drivable, once we get it towed out."

She turns and I catch her smile in the dashboard lights. "Thanks for stopping. I don't know what I would have done." She laughs and adds, "You're my knight in shining armor, or rather, my knight in a down filled jacket and a four-wheel steed with heated seats."

I smile but it scares me to think how easily I could have overlooked her. Thank God I turned my head when I did. "I barely saw you."

She snorts, like I touched on a sore spot. "Yeah, the story of my life."

"What?"

"Nothing. Ignore me. My brain is frozen." She spends a good five minutes trying to undo the knot on the string of her hood. After a few mumbled curses, she gets it undone and pulls it off. I steal another quick glance at her. Holy shit. If someone had told me I was going to rescue the most beautiful woman on the planet, I would have told them they were nuts. Maybe Brandon wasn't lying about the beautiful women, after all. In the dashboard light, I take in her long wavy hair, dark as the night surrounding us.

I force my eyes back on the road—even though I want to keep looking at her longer. How could I have thought she was a guy. From my peripheral vision, I catch the way she fans out her long hair before she ties it into a ponytail. She unzips her coat, and I take in a big sweater that hugs her breasts. She groans as she tugs at her pants.

"Soaked?" I ask.

"Yeah, and all my clothes are in my suitcase, and we know where my suitcase is." Her shoulders sag. "Although I don't think I have any use for a bikini anymore. But we could be stranded for days, and I don't have a change of clothes."

Oh shit, now I'm envisioning her in a bikini.

Concentrate on the road, Chase.

She goes quiet for a moment and stares out the window, deep in thought. What is going through her mind? After a moment, a laugh bubbles out of her, and under her breath she murmurs, "At least I'm in clean underwear."

What the hell?

My throat makes a gurgling sound as I force my thoughts on the road, and not what she's wearing beneath those tight jeans.

Her eyes go wide, and that's when I see her innocence. I let my gaze roam over her face for another split second. There's something very different about her. I think she's giving off a girl-next-door wholesome vibe. At least, this is what I think innocence looks like. I don't see much of it in the puck bunnies who watch us from the bleachers and chase us down after a game.

"Oh, sorry. I don't know why I said that. I guess, it's just... something my mom used to say." She laughs but it's forced. "Always wear clean underwear in case you're in an accident." She shakes her head, like she's flustered. "I mean, I always wear clean underwear. I wasn't suggesting I didn't."

"Oh, sure yeah. I didn't think that at all. I wear clean underwear too."

Why the hell did I say that? Oh, maybe to make this exchange just a little less awkward.

"Oh, God," she mumbles, and shakes her head. While I think she looks adorable, it appears like she wants to jump out of my moving vehicle and run all the way to the motel—or Siberia. She points to her head. "And clearly I'm still suffering from a frozen brain and have no idea what I'm saying."

My gaze sways her way and I glance down at her tight jeans. Jesus, I wish she'd stop rambling on about her underwear, because now I can't stop thinking about what they might look like on her body, or better yet...off.

Isn't this day just getting better and better?

Why yes, yes, it is...

Grab your copy here!

Away Game (Rebels)

ALSO BY CATHRYN FOX

Scotia Storms

Away Game (Rebels)

Warm Up (Rebels)

Crash Course (Rebels)

Home Advantage (Rebels)

Shut Out (Rebels)

Deal Breaker (Rebels)

Moving Target (Rivals)

Face Off (Rivals)

Scoring Fast (Rivals)

Opposing Teams (Rivals)

Hard Burn (Rivals)

Fake Out (Rivals)

End Zone

Fair Play

Enemy Down

Keeping Score

Trading Up

All In

Blue Bay Crew

Demolished

Leveled

Hammered

Single Dad

Single Dad Next Door

Single Dad on Tap

Single Dad Burning Up

Players on Ice

The Playmaker

The Stick Handler

The Body Checker

The Hard Hitter

The Risk Taker

The Wing Man

The Puck Charmer

The Troublemaker

The Rule Breaker

The Rookie

The Sweet Talker

The Heart Breaker

In the Line of Duty

His Obsession Next Door

His Strings to Pull

His Trouble in Talulah

His Taste of Temptation

His Moment to Steal

His Best Friend's Girl

His Reason to Stay

Confessions

Confessions of a Bad Boy Professor

Confessions of a Bad Boy Officer

Confessions of a Bad Boy Fighter

Confessions of a Bad Boy Doctor

Confessions of a Bad Boy Gamer

Confessions of a Bad Boy Millionaire

Confessions of a Bad Boy Santa

Confessions of a Bad Boy CEO

Hands On

Hands On

Body Contact

Full Exposure

Dossier

Private Reserve

House Rules

Under Pressure

Big Catch

Brazilian Fantasy

Improper Proposal

Boys of Beachville

Good at Being Bad

Igniting the Bad Boy

Bad Girl Therapy

Stone Cliff Series:

Crashing Down

Wasted Summer

Love Lessons

Wrapped Up

Eternal Pleasure Series

Instinctive

Impulsive

Indulgent

Sun Stroked Series

Seaside Seduction

Deep Desire

Private Pleasure

Captured and Claimed Series:

Yours to Take

Yours to Teach

Yours to Keep

Firefighter Heat Series

Fever

Siren

Flash Fire

Playing For Keeps Series

Slow Ride

Wild Ride

Sweet Ride

Breaking the Rules:

Hold Me Down Hard

Pin Me Up Proper

Tie Me Down Tight

Stand Alone Title:
Hands on with the CEO
Torn Between Two Brothers
Holiday Spirit
Unleashed
Knocking on Demon's Door
Web of Desire

ABOUT CATHRYN

New York Times and *USA today* Bestselling author, Cathryn is a wife, mom, sister, daughter, and friend. She loves dogs, sunny weather, anything chocolate (she never says no to a brownie) pizza and red wine. She has two teenagers who keep her busy with their never ending activities, and a husband who is convinced he can turn her into a mixed martial arts fan. Cathryn can never find balance in her life, is always trying to find time to go to the gym, can never keep up with emails, Facebook or Twitter and tries to write page-turning books that her readers will love.

Connect with Cathryn:
Newsletter https://app.mailerlite.com/webforms/landing/c1f8n1
Twitter: https://twitter.com/writercatfox
Facebook: https://www.facebook.com/AuthorCathrynFox?ref=hl
Blog: http://cathrynfox.com/blog/
Goodreads: https://www.goodreads.com/author/show/91799.Cathryn_Fox

Pinterest http://www.pinterest.com/catkalen/